KIDSBORO™

Kidsboro

Battle for Control
The Rise and Fall of the Kidsborian Empire
The Creek War
The Risky Reunion

by Marshal Younger

from Adventures in Odyssey®

Tyndale House Publishers, Inc.
Carol Stream, Illinois

A Focus on the Family book published by
Tyndale House Publishers, Inc., Carol Stream, Illinois 60188

Editor: Kathy Davis
Cover design by Joseph Sapulich

Library of Congress Cataloging-in-Publication Data
Younger, Marshal.
The rise and fall of the Kidsborian empire / Marshal Younger.
p. cm. — (Kidsboro ; 2) (Adventures in Odyssey)
Summary: When two boys make up a fake lawsuit, Kidsboro's economy goes into a tailspin, and Ryan must live with the fear that a new boy will reveal a dangerous secret from his past.
ISBN-13: 978-1-58997-410-4
ISBN-10: 1-58997-410-7
[1. Honesty—Fiction. 2. Secrets—Fiction. 3. Conduct of life—Fiction. 4. Christian life—Fiction.] I. Title.
PZ7.Y8943Ris 2007
[Fic]—dc22

2006036538

Printed in the United States of America
1 2 3 4 5 6 7 8 9 / 13 12 11 10 09 08

For Bryn, my firstborn.
The day you were born, the day you were baptized,
and the day you first spelled "photosynthesis" backward,
are still three of the best days of my life.
Thanks for giving those to me.

• • •

ONE

THE MAD AND THE GLAD

SNAP! MAX BROKE THE STICK he was holding. I glanced at him, and he looked at me with narrowed eyes and clenched fists. I couldn't help but smile, and this made him even madder. He glared at me one more time, and then left the crowd to go mourn the end of his reign as the most powerful man in Kidsboro, a community run by kids in Odyssey. Five of us had started Kidsboro months ago and our population had grown. We'd built clubhouses and small businesses in the woods behind Whit's End, an ice cream shop and discovery emporium owned by Mr. John Avery Whittaker, or "Whit" as most adults called him. And I, Ryan Cummings, was the mayor of Kidsboro.

Mark continued his presentation, pulling out a pocketknife and cutting a window out of the tarp. The crowd around him watched with undivided attention. I was the only one who noticed Max leave. I had to follow him. I couldn't help it. I would enjoy seeing him squirm.

Max was forever tricking people out of their money. He always had at least three schemes going at one time. I couldn't understand how he was able to keep up with all of the lies he told.

Because his father owned a construction company, Max had a practically unlimited supply of scrap wood, which he sold to Kidsboro citizens for high prices. Of course, he was paid in Kidsboro money: starbills and tokens.

Max was not only the richest citizen in Kidsboro, he was also the most powerful. No matter how many schemes he pulled, I could never get the city council to kick him out because we needed wood. He could get away with pretty much anything.

But now . . . O glorious day! Now, we had just voted in a new citizen: Mark. His father worked at an awning company. At this very moment, he was showing us how to make the walls of our clubhouses out of plastic tarp instead of wood. Tarp had a lot of advantages over wood. First, there were no cracks that people could see through. Second, it was better for keeping the weather out. Third, it was easier and cheaper to build with.

People loved the idea. If everyone decided to go with the tarp, then we wouldn't need wood anymore and Max would be out of business. Plus, if he tried another one of his schemes and we found out, no one would hesitate to kick him out. At last I could be free of Max.

I caught up to him. "So, Max . . . what do you think about this tarp idea?"

"Go away, Ryan."

"Looks like you may actually have to make an *honest* buck for once."

He stopped suddenly and pointed in my face. "Do you really think I care diddly squat about this tarp guy?"

"It looked like you cared when you demolished that stick back there."

"Let's just keep one thing in mind, partner. The thing that makes me the most powerful man in Kidsboro ain't the wood. It's the fact that I'm 10 times smarter than any of you. This tarp thing is a bump in the road. I'll be back. I'll own this whole place. And when I do . . . you'll be the first person I crush."

He took off toward his home and I didn't follow. I knew he would live up to those words. I was in for a war.

TWO

THE BIG IDEA

MAX'S MELTDOWN WAS THE most exciting thing that had happened in Kidsboro for at least three weeks. School had been out for summer vacation for about a month, and it seemed like we didn't have enough going on to fill up the time. As mayor, one of my duties was to hand in weekly Kidsboro reports to Mr. Whittaker. Lately, he had commented on how boring the entries were.

My daily entries had been getting less and less interesting as the summer wore on. For a couple of days the only thing I had written down was, "I bought a raisin bun at Sid's Bakery."

"It seems like everything has come to a screeching halt," Mr. Whittaker noted.

"I guess we're in a rut. We're all just doing our jobs. Nobody knows what else to do."

"I suppose that's not too much different from real life sometimes. But I certainly didn't think you'd be bored with Kidsboro in just five months."

"What do you think I should do?" I didn't usually ask

this question. As the elected official for Kidsboro, I wanted to solve things on my own instead of asking Mr. Whittaker for advice. He wanted us to solve our own problems too, so for the most part he wasn't involved with running the town. But this was a question I had been mulling over for a week. I figured I could use some help.

"It sounds like you need something to stir things up," he said, scratching his chin. "Maybe a new government project, or a new business, or . . . something the whole town could be involved in."

I agreed with him, but I had no idea what steps to take to make that happen.

• • •

"That's the coolest thing I've ever seen!" my best friend, Scott Sanchez, shouted as the car stopped right in front of him. It was Nelson Swanson's newest invention: a computer-programmable toy car. Eugene Meltsner, a college student and Odyssey's resident genius, had helped Nelson create the car. But he stepped back and allowed Nelson to soak in the limelight.

"Now watch this," Nelson said, kneeling down next to the car. He began to punch numbers into a calculator that was glued to a couple of pieces of plywood on wheels. From the top, it looked very basic. But underneath was a sophisticated system of wires and computer circuits that would boggle the mind of anyone in Kidsboro—except Nelson. "I'm going to program the car to go to Sid's Bakery and return with a donut," he said.

"What?"

"I enter number 12 for Sid's Bakery . . ."

"Um . . . excuse me for living, but," Scott said, "you just tell the car to go to Sid's Bakery, and it knows where it is?"

"I had to preprogram it, of course. You see, yesterday Eugene and I spent all day surveying the dimensions of Kidsboro. I know exactly how many feet specific locations are from this spot right here." He pointed to an X painted on the ground. "So we programmed the car to go 42 feet forward, three feet to the left to get around that tree, and then turn right and go 14 more feet right up to Sid's Bakery."

He looked toward Eugene. Eugene handed him a tiny wagon. "Don't forget to activate the voice player," Eugene whispered to him.

He hooked the wagon onto the back of the car and put three tokens, the price of one donut, into it.

Nelson punched some more buttons and stood up. "Now, instant delivery service."

My mouth fell open as I watched the car go forward 42 feet, turn left and go three feet, and then turn right and go 14 feet. It stopped right in front of Sid's Bakery . . . and beeped its horn! Sid heard the beep and came out of his shop. He looked around confusedly, and then saw the car sitting in front of his door. The car said in Nelson's voice, "Could I have a glazed donut, please?" Sid obeyed without a word, as if this was a customer with arms and legs and absolutely no calculators glued to him. He came back with a glazed donut and placed it in the wagon, taking the tokens in return.

Sid looked around to see if there was a human responsible

for this, and waved when he saw Nelson. He smiled. Now it made sense. We all expected things like this from Nelson. Nelson waved back. His voice came out of the car again, "Press the red button when you are done." Sid obeyed, and the car backed up and retreated along the exact path it had taken to get there. It stopped right in front of Nelson's feet. Nelson casually bent down, picked up his donut, and took a bite.

"Nelson, that's amazing," I said.

"How'd you get it to talk?" Scott asked.

"It's all in the programming."

"It is precisely the same concept as an answering machine," Eugene piped up, obviously unable to control the urge to explain something.

"I can't believe you made that," Scott said to Nelson.

"It's definitely your best invention yet," I added.

"Thanks. I've been working on it for about six months."

"Do you think you could make me one of those?" Scott asked. "I'll pay you for it." I wasn't sure where Scott was going to get the money for this. He was usually broke, but had made a little money with his detective agency during the spring. In a town as small as ours, there wasn't a huge need for a detective, but Scott had actually cracked a couple of cases.

"Sure," Nelson said. "I can have one for you next week." Eugene cleared his throat. Nelson turned and looked at him. "What?"

"Nelson, I believe I will be experiencing a very busy week at the college. Unfortunately, I do not think I'll have much free time to help."

"Oh, okay," Nelson turned back to Scott. "I guess it'll take me a couple of weeks."

"No problem. You know, you could use this car for anything! You could deliver mail with it, or . . ." His eyes lit up. "I could use it in my detective work! I could rig it with a microphone and secretly drive it up to somebody's house and record criminals as they make their plans."

"That would be illegal," I reminded him.

"Who said?"

"It's in the city charter. We have privacy laws." Scott's shoulders drooped.

"You still want the car?" Nelson asked.

"I guess," Scott said.

There were plenty of legal uses for Nelson's car, and I was certain others would see that as well.

• • •

The next night as I was leaving to go to my real home, I was surprised to see a light on in Nelson's clubhouse. Nobody really wanted to hang around town that much at night, because it got awfully dark in the woods. I knocked, but Nelson didn't answer. Thinking he might have left his battery-operated light on accidentally, I opened his door. Nelson was fast asleep. His head was flat on his desk, his glasses pushed over so that his right lens was over his left eye. He was holding a red wire, poised to place it somewhere on the underside of a computerized car on his desk. Four empty cans of caffeine-enriched soda lined a window ledge.

I tapped on his shoulder, first gently, then with more

force. He awoke with a start. "I can't do any more pull-ups!" Nelson shouted and stood up, his face full of utter terror. Obviously, he was having a gym-class nightmare.

"Nelson, it's me."

"What?" he said, straightening his glasses and looking disoriented.

"It's Ryan. You were having a dream."

"Oh." He sat back down at his desk, shook his head, and without missing a beat, put the red wire into a hole near the back end of the car. He began to screw it tight.

"It's late. You need to go home."

"Is it curfew?"

"Pretty close."

"Okay, I'll work until curfew. I'll see you tomorrow."

"How long have you been working on this thing?"

"Since about five . . ." he cleared his throat, "this morning."

"That's . . . 16 hours!"

"I've got it worked out. If I come in here at five o'clock every morning for the rest of the summer, I'll be able to fulfill all the car orders I have by the time school starts back, depending on—"

"Car orders? What do you mean?"

"I did a little demonstration for a group of people yesterday after I showed the car to you. Several of them wanted their own—just like Scott."

"How many?"

"Twelve."

"So you're going to pull 17-hour days until school starts in order to get this done?"

"I'm giving myself Sundays off. And the Fourth of July."

"Are you crazy? You'll be brain dead by August."

"These people are paying top dollar. I could end up as rich as Max."

"How much are you charging?"

"Twenty starbills a car."

My chin dropped. Twenty starbills was an incredible amount of money—and Nelson was planning on making that 12 times over. He could practically buy a *real* car for that. He could buy his own *company* and make . . . Wait a minute! Mr. Whittaker's words flashed into my head.

"Nelson . . . why don't you start your own company?"

"How?"

"With that much money coming in, you could start a factory right here in your clubhouse. You could hire people to do this work *for* you."

"I don't have any money to hire people."

"You could have investors. Ask people for money up front to start your business. Then when you start selling lots of cars, they can share in the huge amounts of money you'll be making."

"So, I could have employees?"

"Sure. Is there anything you could teach other people to do, like attaching the wheels or something?"

"Yes. I mean, with some training, pretty much anybody can do the body work and some of the easier circuitry."

"So, why not?"

Nelson stood up, as if the ideas flying around in his head

had lifted him off his chair involuntarily. He turned to me and smiled.

• • •

And so was born Kidsboro's first mega-business. The next day, Nelson went around to some of the richer citizens of Kidsboro and asked them if they were interested in investing in Nelson Motors, Inc.

"Nelson Motors?"

"Yes," I overheard Nelson say to a potential investor. "I'm planning to start mass-producing the computer cars. I already have 12 orders at 20 starbills apiece."

"What do you need me for?"

"I need your money so I can start the company and hire employees."

"So you want me to give you money."

"Not give. Invest. You see, if you invest in my company, you share in all the money I make off the cars. For example, if you give me 10 starbills right now, I estimate you would get 20 starbills back after I sell my first 12."

"I give you 10, I get back 20. That's it?"

"That's it. And that's just for the first batch. I plan on selling many more after that."

"So I can double my money without doing anything?"

"Absolutely."

This was the pitch Nelson gave to everyone, and it worked! He collected 50 starbills in about two hours. He was ready to start his business.

His search for employees wasn't too difficult either. Everyone liked the idea of making cars. In fact, much to his surprise, several people offered to share their ideas about how to improve the cars. For example, Nelson wasn't too concerned about style, and one of his potential employees offered to make the car look "cooler" with new colors and shapes. He suggested they could even take custom orders. If a customer wanted a race car, a truck, or even a minivan, Nelson Motors would give him exactly what he wanted.

By the end of the week, Nelson had four employees: two builders, one designer, and one tester.

The wheels were rolling—so to speak—both at Nelson Motors and Kidsboro itself.

THREE

TAKING OFF

PEOPLE SAW THE SUCCESS OF Nelson's new business, and suddenly everyone wanted their own. Ideas were popping up everywhere. Jill and Roberto, the editors/reporters of the weekly newspaper, the *Kidsboro Chronicle*, created a new magazine. It would include stories and poems written by Kidsboro citizens, features about people and places in and around Kidsboro, and general interest articles. The first issue included a *Romeo and Juliet*-type short story about a boy falling in love with a girl that his parents didn't like. Jill wrote this story herself, and it was a favorite among the girls in the town, though the boys wanted more "explosions or something." I personally didn't see an appropriate place in the story for a bomb, but I must admit the action did drag a little bit before page 15 or so.

Kidsboro also had a new attraction—a nine-hole miniature golf course created by Mark, the tarp guy. Mark, like every other Kidsboro citizen, had been given a certain amount of Kidsboro money in order to build his house and get established in the community. And by using tarp instead of having to pay Max for wood, he'd had enough money left over to start his business.

Mark bought a piece of property next to his house and brought in some wood to build boundaries and obstacles. He used actual golf balls and clubs. From the way he described it, it sounded like it was going to be one of the favorite activities in Kidsboro.

Then I tried it. He let me play the first round ever. The course went over dirt and around rocks and tree roots. He told me it would be challenging. He didn't want kids to get bored with it too quickly, but he had no idea just how challenging it was. On hole number four, the golfer had to clear the creek to land on the green where the hole was. The green was only about four feet wide—a dinky target. If you hit the ball too softly, it went into the creek. If you hit it too hard, it plummeted down a 15-foot cliff. I, of course, overshot the green and went down the cliff. It took me 18 strokes to get it back up, then the ball went into the creek. Mark just watched and chuckled.

Holes five through nine weren't much better. Hole eight had a working windmill, with turning blades and everything. However, the rotation of the blades was much too fast. If your ball had the misfortune of getting hit by a blade, it would be thrown about 30 feet out of bounds and into the creek. By the end, it had taken me 104 shots to complete the course, a three-hour round of golf. I told Mark I appreciated the challenge, but I was afraid the course might frustrate players more than challenge them. He agreed to take another crack at it.

The most promising new business was the Kidsboro Cineplex: an outdoor movie theater with a small concession stand. Pete, one of two lawyers in town, was a movie buff. His parents owned a huge collection of videos. Mr. Whittaker allowed Pete to use an old video projector that belonged to Whit's End. Pete strung up some bed sheets between trees for the screen, and everyone would bring their own blankets or lawn chairs and watch the movie. It only cost three tokens to get in. Pete had to put up some more sheets to prevent people from peeking in when they hadn't paid. Then he discovered that kids were climbing a nearby tree and watching the movie over the sheets. So Pete hired Alice, our five-foot-eleven policewoman who had biceps thicker than some tree trunks, as a bouncer to keep an eye on the trees around the theater. If she found anybody trying to take a free peek, she would shake the tree until the offender either fell out or surrendered. Pete also hired someone to work at the concession stand, selling popcorn and sodas to moviegoers.

It became a nightly tradition during the summer—every weeknight there would be a new movie and practically everyone in Kidsboro attended. No matter what the movie was, kids would come to the theater just to be with everyone else. It became a time when all of Kidsboro came together as a sort of family. It made me proud to be a citizen.

The only problem was that at the end of the movie every night, Pete would hold a discussion about the film. I think he mainly did this to show off his impressive film vocabulary. One night, after watching a mindless movie about a guy whose family is taken hostage by bad guys while he's in the garage (as it turns out, he bests them with a weed whacker), the discussion among the boys became quite passionate.

"That was so cool when the trailer blew up!"

"The hero was awesome!"

"That was an incredible fight at the end!"

"Great movie, man!"

Then Pete took the floor and announced, "The cinematography was a bit uninspired," and went on and on about it. This, of course, took the wind out of the sails of anyone who had actually enjoyed the film. This happened pretty much every night. The crowd would talk about how much they loved the movie, and then Pete would get up and explain why the editing was uneven or whatever. It was actually getting a little annoying. Then one night someone finally had the guts to challenge him.

"I found the Jane character to be one-dimensional," Pete said. "She was merely a piece of cardboard. And what was the point of having the grandmother come back? I found that to be a very implausible plot twist."

"Oh, yeah?" came a voice out of the crowd. "You think you can do any better?"

Pete was totally thrown off by this. No one ever challenged him. "What?"

"You haven't liked a single movie you've shown here. So why don't you make one yourself?"

Pete's body twisted and it looked as if he was going to lose his balance. "Well . . . I'm not a filmmaker."

"You act like it," the boy said as others nodded.

"I don't have the equipment . . ."

"Your dad has a video camera, right?"

"Yes."

"You've got a whole town full of people who can be your actors. What else do you need?"

Pete swallowed and looked out at the crowd. He took a deep breath, and then nodded. "Okay. I will. I *will* make a movie." Suddenly, he stood up straight and, as if he were announcing his candidacy for president, said, "And it'll be better than anything you've seen so far."

The crowd was both excited and skeptical. It was certainly a fun prospect to be involved in a movie.

And so began a new industry in Kidsboro: filmmaking.

FOUR

BLACKMAIL

I WAS WALKING TOWARD MY office when someone snuck up from behind and tricked me.

"Jim!" he shouted.

On impulse, I turned around. I immediately wished I hadn't.

"Gotcha!" he said, laughing. It was Jake Randall—a face from the past I had hoped was out of my life forever. "I knew you were Jim."

"My name's not Jim," I said. "It's Ryan."

"But you turned your head when I called you Jim."

I had to think fast, before he noticed how nervous I was. "You were 10 feet behind me and you screamed something. I would've turned around no matter what name you called."

"What a lie," he said, bumping me with his shoulder.

He was right. I was lying, but I had good reason. My real name was Jim Bowers, and he was the only one in Kidsboro who knew it. I had known Jake since we were kids in California, before I moved to Odyssey. There was a secret surrounding my life in California, and Jake knew some of it. Now he was spending his summer in Odyssey, harassing me here just as he had done in California. Since the day I had run into him again after four years, I had tried to act like I didn't know what he was talking about when he called me Jim. But he knew my real name, and he knew I was running away from it. He didn't know everything—at least I didn't *think* he knew everything. I had to prevent him from finding out the whole truth. It would be too dangerous for my family.

I continued walking toward my office. I was hoping he would go the other way. He didn't.

"I've heard about this nice little . . . like . . . *town* you've got here. Cute little clubhouses everywhere. And I hear you're the mayor or something?"

"Yes."

"How many people have you got livin' here?"

"Thirty."

"Wow. Congrats. Leader of 30 people—five months before you're even a teenager." He leaned down and whispered in my ear, "Notice how I know your exact age?"

"Good guess. Maybe you can get a job at a carnival."

"Yeah, this little town's nice and comfy. Got a bakery, a newspaper . . . I ran into your police chief back there. That girl's a tank." He was referring to Alice, of course.

"I wouldn't say that to her face."

"You think I'm nuts?"

"You know," I said, "I have some things to do. I'll see you around." I sped up and ducked my head into my office. He didn't take the hint. He followed me in.

He sat down in a chair and put his feet up on my desk. "I

was thinking about maybe becoming a citizen myself. Where do I sign up?"

For the first time, I looked directly at him. My veins turned to ice. If Jake became a citizen, I wouldn't be able to sleep at night. I would be constantly looking over my shoulder and checking behind trees.

"You know, it's pretty hard to get in," I said. "You have to go through a screening process, and you have to win an 80 percent majority vote in the city council. It's not really up to me."

"I see," he said. "So, you don't think I have a chance?"

"Well . . . you're new here. I don't really know you, and I don't think anyone else on the council does either. It might be a long shot."

"But you're the mayor. You can make things work out for me, right? Or don't you want to?" I didn't answer. "You know what? I've got something that might make you want to. Come with me."

"Look . . . *Jake,* is it? I don't have the time. Maybe . . ."

"I think you're gonna want to see this." I looked up and saw him smiling. He had me. I didn't know how, but he had me. I was compelled to follow him. Without a word, he headed for the movie theater. Pete was setting up for that night's feature. We stepped across the series of extension cords that led from the woods to Whit's End and approached him.

"Ask him if we could use the video projector for a bit." I did, and Pete agreed. He turned the power on, and then went back into his office/house. Jake and I were alone.

Jake pushed a videocassette labeled "Tenth Birthday"

into the projector. "After our last little encounter, I did some research. I had my mom send me this video from California. I think you'll find it very interesting."

The screen lit up and showed a birthday party. The cake said *Happy 10th Birthday, Jake,* and in the background was a 10-year-old Jake. He puffed up his cheeks and blew out the candles as everyone clapped. Then the camera panned and caught a little boy wearing a purple superhero shirt—an eight-year-old me. The person operating the camera said, "Jim! Make your funny face." The eight-year-old me scrunched up his face as though he had just eaten a box of lemons. Jake pressed the pause button, crossed his arms, and glared at me.

"You know," Jake said, "that kid looks . . . like . . . *exactly* like you. But . . . they called him Jim. I wonder why."

"I guess his name is Jim," I said as calmly as I could. "I admit, he sure looks like me. Thanks for showing me that. It was interesting." I started to head back to my office.

"You want to see another coincidence?" he said, stopping me in my tracks. He pressed a button and the video started up again. I was still making faces, and there, coming up from behind me, was my mom. She hugged my neck. Then she looked right into the camera and the two of us smiled. Ten-year-old Jake came into the picture and called her "Mrs. Bowers."

"You see, that's what's weird," Jake said. "That kid's mother looks just like *your* mother. And yet her name is Mrs. Bowers. Can you believe that coincidence?" He paused for effect. "No. You don't believe that's a coincidence. And neither will anybody else. Can you imagine how awful it would be if, for some reason, this tape accidentally got switched with the tape Pete's going to play at the Cineplex tonight? You would have a lot of explaining to do, huh?"

The tape was still rolling. There were only five or six kids at the party that day. Jake was not real popular. He had invited me only because he had very few other friends. My mom and I were sitting together as we watched Jake open his presents. I got excited when he opened the one I gave him—one of those super water guns. Jake immediately ran to the bathroom to fill it up. I smiled at my mom and said, "I told you he'd like it." Times were much simpler then.

"So what's your story, Jim? Why are you hiding out here with a bogus name? It's not because you're scared of *me*, is it? Surely you don't think I'm still mad about that whole detention center thing."

Just a few months after that birthday party, Jake had taken me out to the woods and showed me his father's gun. I got scared, and I ran and told my mom. She called the police, and they came and picked him up. Of course, the gun episode hadn't been the only reason Jake had been sent away, but I sensed he blamed me anyway.

"Surely you didn't move away just because I had to spend the next three months in a juvenile detention center." Jake said. He was telling me now, four years later, that he wasn't mad about it. But I couldn't imagine that he had put it behind him. I was sure he wanted revenge.

"You know what? I don't think that's it," he said. "This is a long way to come just to get away from me. I think you ran away from California for a different reason." I swallowed a lump in my throat. "It was a weird thing. Nobody in our old neighborhood could figure it out. You and your mom just suddenly disappeared. Not even your father knew where you were." He smiled. "I think you were running away from *him*."

He knew it all. When I was eight, my mother and I gathered up our belongings and left the house in the middle of the night to escape an abusive husband and father—my dad. If he had known we were leaving, or where we were going, he would've found us and maybe hurt us even worse than he had before. He was an alcoholic and we never knew how violent he would turn at any given moment when he was drinking. So we left that night and went to an abuse shelter, where they helped us start our lives over. They gave us new names, a new address thousands of miles away, and a new life. They told us not to tell anyone in Odyssey about our past, not even our closest friends. Now . . . my worst enemy knew.

"Jake, you can't tell anybody."

"Oh, I don't plan to. You know, as long as you keep me happy."

He had me. I had to give him whatever he wanted.

"What do you want?" I asked him.

"I want to be a citizen."

"Why?"

"I haven't gotten to know many people here. I think it'd be nice to settle down in a small town . . ." This part I believed. Jake was never one to make friends easily. But I didn't believe this was the only reason he wanted to be a part of my town.

"I told you, it's not completely my decision," I told him.

"Then you'd better hope your friends follow your lead and vote for me."

"They don't even know you."

"Tell them about me. Tell them what a good pal I've always been to you." In other words, lie.

"I can't guarantee anything," I said.

"Sure you can."

"I'll do my best."

"That's the spirit."

But don't ask me any questions, I thought. *You don't need to know anything else.*

• • •

I rolled back over onto my stomach. I could never sleep on my stomach, but I wasn't sleeping anyway. I thought about waking Mom up and telling her everything, but I didn't want her to panic and insist that we move out of Odyssey. I liked it here.

I also considered telling Mr. Whittaker. He was the only person in Odyssey besides my mom and I who knew the truth about our situation. When we moved to Odyssey, we immediately knew he was a person we could trust. He helped us out a lot, and was responsible for my mother and me becoming Christians. I wanted to tell him, but I knew he would want me to tell my mom, and I didn't want her to worry. Why did Jake have to show up and ruin everything?

I couldn't imagine Jake being a citizen of Kidsboro—to look across the way and see Jake eating a donut from Sid's

Bakery, attending a movie at the Cineplex, talking with all of my real friends. I would be constantly wondering what the topic of conversation was . . .

I would have to look straight into the faces of the city council members and tell them that Jake would be a wonderful asset to our community. I had no choice.

• • •

I called a city council meeting first thing the next morning. Everyone was there—Scott, Nelson, Alice, Jill, and me. None of them knew why I had called the meeting.

"I want to vote in another citizen," I said, my stomach turning.

As I expected, Jill immediately objected, "I thought we were going to stop at 30 for the rest of the summer."

"That's right. We did say that at the last meeting," Alice agreed.

"Then someone must be leaving," Nelson said.

"Who's leaving?" Scott asked.

"No one's leaving. There's just someone I think we should consider."

"Who?"

I took a long breath. "Do you guys know Jake Randall?" I got blank stares.

"Never heard of him," Scott said.

"He's from California. He's visiting for the summer—staying with his grandmother or something."

"He doesn't live here?" Jill asked with an exaggerated shrug of her shoulders.

"No, he doesn't. But I think he could turn into a very valuable citizen."

"Why?" Jill asked.

"Because," I could tell that I hadn't rehearsed this well enough. "Because . . . he's . . . smart . . ."

"That's it? He's smart?"

"No, that's not it."

Jill wasn't going to let up. "Well, you're going to have to make a better case for him than that. None of us knows the guy. How do you expect us to vote for him?"

Alice spoke up. "Can we ask some questions about him?"

"Sure."

"Does he have a record?" she asked, without a hint of a smile.

"You mean, is he a *criminal*?" Did Alice have a sense about these things, or was this just a standard question? I didn't answer.

"Do you mind if I do a check on him?"

"Um . . . no, go ahead."

Alice wrote something down in the notebook she kept in her shirt pocket.

"You say," Nelson said, "we could benefit from him being a citizen. How?"

"How? Well . . . like I said, he's smart. I could see him starting a new business."

"We have tons of new businesses."

"True. You're right, we do. But . . . his business could really . . ." I looked around at the confused faces around me.

They weren't buying it. I didn't want to resort to this, but I had run out of options.

"Listen," I began, swallowing a lump in my throat, "do you think you could maybe just . . . trust me on this one?" Jill and Nelson exchanged looks while Alice and Scott stared at me through squinted eyes. "I can't explain right now. I just . . . need for you to vote for this guy. Okay?"

There was silence as I scanned the faces of my friends. Jill looked down, fiddled with her ear, and finally said, "Okay. I trust you. I'll vote for him."

"Me too," Scott said. Nelson and Alice followed.

"All right then," I said sheepishly. "Jake's a citizen." I let out an unintentional sigh of relief and Jill glanced at me. "Thanks. Meeting adjourned."

"Do we get to meet Jake at some point?" Jill asked.

"Sure. Um . . . he'll be around. I'll introduce him." We all filed out.

As I headed back to my office, I noticed that Jill and Scott had remained in the meeting hall. When I looked back, they saw me, and their conversation came to an abrupt halt. They both gave me an awkward smile and pretended, badly, that nothing was going on. I turned back around and tried to act like I wasn't affected by this scene, but I had a feeling that their level of trust in me had taken a hit.

• • •

I hadn't attended the Kidsboro Community Church for several weeks, but I decided to go, hoping that Reverend

Joey might say something to inspire me. When I arrived, he and Mr. Whittaker were the only ones there. Joey preached, banged his fist on the music stand a couple of times, and led us in a couple of songs. With the Fourth of July coming up, I think he preached on appreciating America. To be honest, I wasn't paying much attention. It was when he asked if anyone wanted to come to the altar to pray that I woke up.

I walked up to where Joey had laid out a couple of milk crates for an altar. I knelt down and almost started to cry. I felt terrible for deceiving people that I really cared about.

"Lord, please forgive me for lying. But I don't know what to do. I don't want to keep lying, but I can't tell them the truth, either," I whispered.

Mr. Whittaker startled me with a tap on the shoulder. "Are you okay, Ryan?" I wanted to tell him everything, but I couldn't.

"I'm okay."

"Would you like me to pray with you?"

"No. I'd just like to pray alone for now."

"Okay, Ryan. But let me know if you need to talk." He hesitated, waiting for me to take him up on his offer. Seeing that I wasn't going to at this point, he slowly backed away.

I finished my prayer with one more sentence, "Please, God, show me what I can do."

I didn't get an answer immediately, but I figured one was coming. God had never let me down before.

• • •

Jake was all smiles when the city council greeted him as the newest citizen of Kidsboro. He was building his house very close to my office, and the sight of it gave me an instant headache. I stood at a distance while Jill, Scott, Nelson, and Alice shook his hand, one by one.

The only good thing about this scene was the fact that Jake's house would be the second to use tarp, thus continuing the demise of Max's chokehold on the city.

• • •

Even though Jake was now a citizen of Kidsboro, I couldn't help but smile when I saw how far the town had come in such a short time. Everywhere I looked, people were involved in businesses of various kinds. Pete had no problem finding investors for his movie. Just as with Nelson's cars, we all knew the movie would make a lot of money. Everyone figured that people would pay to see it simply to watch themselves onscreen. Pete raised 40 starbills almost immediately. That would be plenty to pay all the actors and crew members.

But I also noticed that something disturbing was going on. People who couldn't get investors for their businesses were borrowing money from each other. I didn't like this going on between friends, because if someone couldn't pay a friend back, it might hurt the friendship.

So I discussed an idea with the city council: We needed to start a bank. "People will put their extra money in the bank, so they can earn interest. Interest is money the bank pays you because it gets to use your money for a while. It's a form of investing. I figure people will go for it because they will be making money for doing nothing," I explained.

"On the flip side, people can also *borrow* money from the bank if they want to start new businesses. On a loan, they'll have to *pay* interest. The longer they take to pay back their loans, the more money they'll have to pay back. Hopefully, once the borrowers get their businesses going, they'll be making enough money to pay back their loans pretty easily."

Everyone on the city council agreed it was time for Kidsboro to open a bank.

• • •

As soon as we announced the opening of the Kidsboro Savings and Loan, people began to gather up their extra cash and deposit it in the bank. I appointed Marcy to be the bank teller. She had always had trouble finding a job, plus she had a laptop computer, so she was a natural choice. Nelson brought his newfound wealth and deposited all of it. Before lunch, a total of 182 starbills had been deposited into the bank. Once there were funds in the bank, people were able to take out loans to start their own businesses. And from the crowd of people outside the bank that first day, it looked like the bank was turning out to be a good idea.

FIVE

THE GOLDEN ERA

I TOOK A LOOK AT Pete's movie script before the filming started. Not that I could've stopped him from making the film, but I told him I wanted to see the script so that I could decide whether or not I could support it as mayor. I didn't want the citizens of Kidsboro imitating Hollywood morals in one of its own productions.

I was pleased to discover that everything in it seemed harmless. The plot was fun and exciting. It might not be a classic, but I wouldn't withhold my support just because I thought it wasn't going to win any awards.

Pete held auditions for all the roles in his film. He told everyone that it was an action/adventure movie and that there were plenty of parts to audition for. Anyone who did not get an acting role could be hired as a crew person—cameraman, assistant director, sound technician (microphone holder, as it turned out), and so on. Practically everyone in Kidsboro showed up to audition. I sat and watched part of it, though I didn't audition myself. Pete sat in a director's chair. He had on sunglasses and held a megaphone, though it was an overcast day and he was only 15 feet away from the actors.

"Next," Pete said through his megaphone. Scott stepped to the front. "Name?" Pete asked.

"You know my name," Scott said.

"Name?" Pete insisted.

Scott rolled his eyes. "Scott Sanchez."

Pete wrote something down in his notebook. "Is that with an *S*?"

"Yes, two of them."

"And what part will you be reading for?"

"I'll be reading for the part of Rock Bockner."

"Oh . . ." Pete said, shaking his head. "I'm sorry, I've already cast that part."

Scott instantly objected, "Well, excuse me for using up oxygen, but am I not the first guy to audition? How could you have cast the part already?"

"It was a pre-production decision. Why don't you try out for Dead Guy number two?"

"Who got the part of Rock?" Scott demanded. At this point, other guys who were waiting their turn moved in to see what was going on.

Pete noticed the sudden invasion. "Would all other auditioners wait behind the curtain, please?"

"We want to know who got the part of Rock!" one boy demanded.

"Rock Bockner is . . ." Pete began quietly, then with all the confidence he could muster, he looked him straight in the eyes. "Me."

The boys immediately burst into hysterical laughter. Pete looked offended. "What's wrong with that?"

"Rock Bockner is not a four foot nine, 87-pound ostrich. He's a big, tough guy. With muscles and . . . a cool haircut," somebody responded.

"I can pull it off," Pete said.

"My sister could play Rock Bockner better than you."

This went on for another few minutes until Pete put his director's hat back on and insisted that they move on.

• • •

Auditions continued for the next couple of hours. The boys all came desiring the role of Rock and had their hopes dashed. But the best girl's part was still up for grabs. It was the role of Ginger, Rock's love interest and leading lady. Pete got to live out the dreams of pretty much every teenage boy in Odyssey—to choose from a long line of girls exactly who got to be his love interest.

At 1:13 that afternoon, the girls who were still standing in line realized they had no hope of being Ginger when they saw Valerie Swanson take her place in the audition chair. Like most of the guys in town, Pete was secretly in love with Valerie. She sat down and read for the part, but he never heard a word she said. He just stared at her with his chin resting sloppily in his hand. After she was done he said, "Wonderful." She smiled, flipped her hair back, and left.

• • •

After the main characters were cast, Pete held auditions for stuntmen. A dozen boys lined up to do whatever Pete asked, unconcerned with the danger. To refuse a challenge in front of a crowd of other boys would be unthinkable.

At one point Pete said, "All right, line up and jump off this cliff." The drop was about 10 feet. The landing didn't appear to be terribly dangerous, but no one knew if there were rocks beneath the surface of the dirt. "Who's first?" Pete asked as he took his chair and notebook down to the bottom of the cliff. Everyone casually shuffled backwards to allow someone else to go first. "Come on, people!" Pete shouted. "You can't be a stuntman if you're afraid to do what I tell you."

The boys looked at each other. They were hoping to find a hint of fear in one another's eyes so that they knew they were not alone. Finally, Scott, whom everyone knew didn't have a courageous bone in his body, asked a question that everyone would love him for. "Can we have some pillows down there?"

"Pillows?" Pete said.

"Yeah," Scott went on. "Whenever stuntmen jump off buildings and stuff, they always get one of those big balloon things to land on. I figured at least we could get some pillows." Some of the others nodded in agreement, casually shrugging their shoulders. No one wanted to admit that they needed pillows.

Pete rolled his eyes and sent a boy to get pillows. "Does

anybody want to really impress me and do it without the pillows?" Pete challenged. But everyone collectively agreed to wait for the pillows.

The boy came back with a pile of laundry. "My mom wouldn't let me have pillows, but she gave me some old beach towels."

Towels? I didn't think towels would absorb much of the shock. It was, after all, a 10-foot drop. Pete laid the towels out on the ground, covering a fairly wide area at the bottom of the cliff. All in all, the towels appeared to provide about an inch and a half of padding.

Pete patted the towels, showing the prospective jumpers just how nice and soft the ground was now. He looked up at them, then backed into his director's chair. "All right. Who's first?"

They all looked at each other. "Scott," Pete said, "you got your padding. Why don't you give it a try?" Scott scratched the back of his neck and took a step forward to look over the cliff. He licked his lips and clenched his teeth.

"All right, everybody back up," Scott said. They obeyed. He backed up 20 feet and took a deep breath. The other boys were in awe. He closed his eyes, took a running start, and hurled himself off the cliff. He let out a small squeal and landed on the edge of the towels, fell awkwardly, and took a violent turn to the right, rolling into the bushes. He screamed in pain. Pete ran over to him, and the other boys peered over the top of the cliff to see what damage had been done.

"Are you okay?" Pete asked. Scott's eyes were closed. He grunted a bit and gingerly pulled a branch away from his face. He wiggled his toes as if to test for paralysis. Pete scanned his body for blood, but saw none. "Do you want me to help you up?"

Scott said with difficulty, "I'm okay."

"Anything broken?" Pete asked.

"I don't think so."

"Here. Let me help you," Pete said, grabbing his arm.

"No!" Scott shouted. "I got the wind knocked out of me. I'll just stay here for now."

"Under the bush?"

"Sure."

"You want me to just leave you here?"

"Yeah. I'll be fine."

Pete looked up at the boys at the top of the cliff. He walked to his chair. "Okay, good. Who's next?"

The boys looked at each other, waved a group good-bye, and went home. Pete went back over to Scott, who hadn't moved. "Congratulations, Scott. You're our stuntman."

• • •

On the way back into town the next morning, I noticed something very odd and disturbing. Jake's new house was not made of tarp, as I thought it would be. It was made of wood, just like everyone else's. Why would somebody pay top dollar to buy wood from Max when he could have a perfectly good house made of tarp for much less?

I got my answer seconds later. Max came up from behind me.

"Hey, Ryan. I met your buddy Jake." I practically bit my tongue in half. "I hear you guys go way back," he said.

"What did he tell you?" I asked, hoping he didn't notice the tremble in my voice.

"Just that you two have a special bond between you that goes back to your kindergarten days. Nice guy."

"Sure is."

"I look forward to getting to know him. In fact, he may just turn out to be one of my best friends." He winked at me and left. The lump in my throat was so large that I couldn't swallow. Max never wanted to get to know anyone. He didn't care about having friends. Why would he want to be Jake's friend? And why did Jake agree to buy Max's wood? Did Max give him the wood at a special price in exchange for . . . *information*? I could handle Max most of the time. Jake would be tougher, but I still thought I could deal with him. But the two of them together . . .

• • •

I expected the first day of filming to be like a soccer practice for five year olds—one person trying to organize 10 other people who would rather just kick stuff around. But when I got there, I was amazed to see that Pete had everything under control. In fact, he looked as though he knew exactly what he was doing every step of the way.

He had his lead actors in place. Valerie was standing behind the camera, ready to go on set. A boy named Kirk had won the part of the bad guy. He was wearing a black suit and he had a smirk on his face. His longer hair gave him a convincing bad-guy look.

Pete had put the camera tripod on wheels and bought some plywood from Max so that he could easily roll the camera, making a sort of makeshift dolly. He watched through the viewfinder and yelled "Action!"

Kirk was already on the set, sitting at a table in what looked like an outdoor café. Valerie approached him cautiously. She spoke with a hint of fear in her voice. "What do you want?"

"Thanks for coming, Ginger. Have a seat." She sat down. Pete whispered something to his cameraman and motioned to two production assistants standing nearby. They wheeled the dolly slowly to the left.

"I want the computer disk," Kirk said.

"What if I don't have it?"

Kirk laughed. Pete had the cameraman move in slowly. "Well, then . . . I guess I don't have your mother, either."

Valerie gasped. "What have you done with my mother?"

"The question should be, 'What will we do to your mother if you don't comply?' And the answer, for now, is that we haven't done anything . . . yet. She's safe and sound and could remain that way, but that's up to you."

Pete signaled to a guy who was operating a large fan. A fairly heavy breeze suddenly hit the scene and Valerie's hair fluttered. Then Pete motioned to Patty, who was off-camera. She approached with a tray full of food in one hand, and a plastic pitcher of water in the other.

"The shrimp looks good," Kirk said, seeing the tray.

Valerie didn't care about the shrimp. "What's to prevent me from going to the police right now?"

"Oh, I don't think you want to deal with the police. Not with *your* past, Ginger . . . or should I say . . . *Gretchen*." Valerie gasped again. She was really good at that. She exhaled, and then pushed her hair back casually as if to mask her fear. Suddenly, she glanced upward. Her eyes widened when she saw Patty, the waitress. The wind from the fan had blown a large oak leaf into her face, and it had stuck there. She was powerless to do anything because both her hands were full. Valerie snickered a little, but quickly looked away. Patty was jerking her head to the left, trying to get the leaf off, but it remained stuck.

Kirk noticed Valerie's snicker and looked up at Patty. He made a funny noise, then grabbed his water glass and drank. Valerie and Kirk tried to regain their composure and continue with the scene. Charlie, the guy holding the microphone, noticed the leaf and tried to stifle his laughter, but the microphone began shaking above Kirk's head. Pete saw the microphone and the sudden change in the actors, and he looked around. He finally noticed the leaf that appeared to be a part of Patty's face. She swung the pitcher up toward her face to scrape it off, but instead the water flew up out of the pitcher and spilled over the front of her shirt. She remained calm. Pete bowed his head and his body shook with laughter.

Heroically, the actors continued on. "You see, Ginger . . ." Kirk said with a slight smile, "we have many ways of getting that disk, even if you don't give it to us."

Valerie covered her mouth and was barely able to deliver her line. "What are you talking about?"

"Well . . . we could . . . we could . . ." He was starting to lose it. "We could glue a leaf to your face just like we did to her!"

The entire cast and crew burst into hysterics. Patty grinned, threw the plastic pitcher down, and peeled the leaf off her face. Valerie and Kirk laughed until they cried. Pete fell on the ground headfirst. I had to hold my side to keep it from bursting. Valerie stood up and gave Patty a sympathy hug. Patty laughed at herself.

After five full minutes of utter frenzy, Pete began to get everything set up again. The crew went back to their places, Patty reloaded her tray and pitcher, and no one was upset that they had to do the entire scene over again.

It was one of the nicest moments in the history of Kidsboro.

• • •

I left the set for a while and took a leisurely walk around. There were several people playing on the miniature golf course. Mark had made a few changes in the course. It was actually possible to make a decent score on a couple of the holes.

Nelson, Eugene, and two employees were giving their newest model a road test: a stylish, red pickup truck. He'd gotten several more orders for this model. Nelson had a stack of wood nearby, and the truck had a small stack in its bed. Eugene had a pencil behind his ear and a pad in his hand. He was smiling as though he was impressed. Apparently, they were testing to see how much weight the truck would hold.

I stopped by the bank, and Marcy was signing a few papers. A customer was opening up a new account. Marcy explained the concept behind interest, withdrawals, and deposits. She entered some figures into her computer.

I went into my office, sat back in my chair, and smiled. I was proud of my city. This was how it was supposed to be.

Suddenly, the door crashed open and Scott burst in. "There's been an accident!"

SIX

THE BEGINNING OF THE END

SEVERAL PEOPLE WERE ALREADY AT the scene when I got there. Jill, the newspaper reporter, was there with her notebook and pen. Roberto, assistant newspaper editor/reporter/photographer, was taking pictures of the scene. And lying on the ground, holding his ankle, was Jake. James, the town doctor, was kneeling down beside him with his medical bag. I suppose I should have asked Jake if he was okay, but I couldn't bring myself to do it.

He offered the information on his own. "I think I pulled something."

James fumbled around in his bag. He had never actually treated anyone, so he looked excited to finally get a chance to use his limited knowledge of first aid. He pulled out an Ace bandage.

"Let's wrap that—"

"Get away from me, you quack!" Jake shouted.

"What happened?" Jill asked.

"I fell on one of Nelson's stupid cars. It came out of nowhere and I tripped over it."

"Can you walk?" Scott asked.

"I haven't tried."

Scott and James helped Jake up, and he tried to walk on his own. His ankle buckled and he almost fell. They gently helped him sit back down.

Nelson ran up. "What's going on?"

"You!" Jake screamed. "You and your stupid cars!"

"My cars?"

"I fell over one! And I might've torn something."

"I'm sorry . . ." Nelson noticed one of his cars upside down on the grass. He turned it over and saw that the entire length of the car had been crushed. He went over to help Jake.

"Don't even come near me! Haven't you done enough?"

"Jake, I'm just trying to help. It's not my fault that you fell on the car."

"And why not?"

"Who was driving it?"

"I don't know. But you're the one who invented these death-mobiles."

"That's irrelevant."

"It's *your* fault. And I'm gonna take you for every penny you've got."

"What?" Nelson asked with his eyes open as big as saucers.

"I'm suing you," Jake said. Nelson stepped back as if he was going to faint. Kidsboro had gotten sue-happy before, and it had hurt the town badly. I didn't want to go through that again.

"Now come on, Jake," Nelson said. "You don't need to sue me."

"What do you care? You're rich."

Scott went to get Mr. Whittaker, who rushed out the back door of his shop, and down the main street of Kidsboro. He bent down at Jake's side. "Can you walk?"

"No."

"Where does it hurt?"

"I'm okay. I just need to get home."

Mr. Whittaker pulled Jake up, threw his arm around him, and half-carried him off. Jake moaned until he was out of earshot.

• • •

The whole story was in the *Kidsboro Chronicle* the next day, along with a picture of the scene of the accident, some quotes from Jake, "our newest citizen," and comments from Nelson. Jake's threat to sue Nelson "for every penny" was in there too. I was hoping that part of the story wouldn't appear in the paper.

I didn't want anyone to think there was any kind of trouble in paradise during this "golden age" of Kidsboro, as I liked to call it. But now it was out there, and all I could do was hope that it wouldn't lead to anything worse.

• • •

"Come on! I've been behind the camera for an hour and a half, and I haven't even filmed anything yet!" Pete's cameraman complained. It had been a long day and tempers appeared to be running high. This was the fifth day in a row they had been filming.

"Hang on," Pete answered. "I just have to work some things out." Pete was explaining the next scene to Stuntman Scott.

"Okay, you're being chased by Kirk. You've got the disk in your pocket and you're trying to get it to Rock. Over by the creek, you jump on your getaway bike, and you have this high-speed bike chase through the woods. Kirk will be behind you. When you get over here, you lose control of your bike and run into this tree right here."

"What?"

"And make sure you hit the jagged branches."

"You want me to run into a tree?"

"Yes."

"At full speed?"

"Yes."

"On an out-of-control bike?"

"Yes."

"Excuse me for being sane, but are you crazy?"

"Are you not my stuntman?"

"Sure, but . . . don't you think that's kind of dangerous?"

"What? You want me to nail some pillows to the tree?" Pete asked, throwing his arms up in disbelief.

Scott thought a minute, then said quietly, "Yes."

Pete looked disgusted. "We can't put pillows on the trees; the camera will pick them up. Now if you want to remain my stuntman, I suggest you get on that bike and start plummeting headfirst into that tree!"

Scott put his head down and headed for the bike. Several times he turned back and glanced at the tree as though wondering how to escape certain discomfort.

As Scott prepared for his big scene, Valerie came over with a script in her hand. She was as fed up as everyone else seemed to be.

"What is this?" she asked Pete.

Pete looked at where she was pointing on the script, acting as if he had no idea what she was talking about. But he obviously knew what she was going to complain about.

"What?"

She began reading from the script, "'Rock gently pulls her toward him and kisses her on the lips. Ginger knows she must resist, but cannot. She melts into his powerful arms.'" She looked up. "I am *not* kissing you, nor am I melting into your powerful, yet completely unmuscular, arms."

"But . . . Valerie . . ." Pete responded with all the confidence he could muster. "It's very important to the script. This is a turning point for your character. Ginger has never let herself become vulnerable before. Now she's falling in love and has no choice. She has to trust him."

"I think I can communicate that in other ways."

"Like what?"

"I don't know. I'll give Rock a little thumbs-up sign or something."

"Dramatically, that's a little less impressive than what I was going for."

"I know what you were going for," Valerie said suspiciously. "I'm not kissing you, and that's final."

"Do you want this to be a good movie or not?"

"More importantly, I will have a *life* after this movie. And I would like to be able to sleep at night and not have nightmares about your disgusting little lips coming at me."

"You know, I don't want to pull rank, but who's the artist here?"

"Are you kidding me? You call this art?" Valerie turned back a page in the script and pointed to a selection. "This line, right here. This line that you are expecting me to memorize and say on camera. *This* is art?"

Pete scanned it. "That's *beautiful*. It's practically *poetry*!"

"This is garbage! Listen to this, everyone." She began reading, "'Rock, ever since I met you the stars seem to shine brighter, the mountains seem taller . . . flowers seem to smell sweeter. I love you because of the way you make me feel, Rock.'"

"You don't like that?"

"That's *terrible*!"

"You're just so used to your soap operas that when you see a well-written love story, you don't even recognize it."

"I guarantee you I could write better than this."

"Then be my guest, Valerie! *You* rewrite that scene, and we'll see how artistic you and your little soap-opera brain can be."

"Love to." Valerie closed the script and headed off to work on the rewrite. Pete shook his head back and forth violently to illustrate to everyone around him how frustrating actors can be.

With that over, Pete got ready for the bike-chase scene.

Scott was ready, and Pete gave the signal for the cameraman to roll.

Scott took a deep breath and started pedaling. He veered toward the tree he was preparing to hit. Kirk started up behind him.

"Faster!" Pete called out. Scott stood up on his pedals to gain more speed. Kirk came up behind him.

"You're too close together!" Pete yelled. "Speed up, Scott!"

Scott obeyed again. He clenched his teeth and looked directly at the tree.

"Now look back a couple of times, like you're scared he's catching up!"

Scott glanced toward Kirk and swerved around a rock. There was nothing between him and the tree now.

"Faster!" Pete shouted. Scott pedaled faster, and it really did look like he was starting to lose control. I put my hand over my mouth and prepared for the impact.

Scott closed his eyes, hit a root, and lost control of the handlebars, swerving to the right and crashing into the tree at an angle. His left leg hit sharply against the bark, sending him flying out of the seat. The bike flipped and fell on top of him. The back wheel pinned his leg to the ground. Scott lay motionless, the front wheel still spinning.

Everyone nearby ran toward him.

"Are you okay?" I asked.

Scott opened his eyes. He breathed heavily, glancing around at all the faces staring down at him. "I'm fine," he said.

"Fantastic!" Pete shouted after seeing that Scott was still alive. "Wonderful, Scott. Now let's go to another angle and do it again."

Scott's eyes opened wide. "You're crazy," he said, still lying on his back. "I'm not doing that again."

"We have to get it from another angle, so that we have something to cut to," Pete said, as though Scott should understand this logic.

"Forget it, Pete. I quit."

"Come on, Scott, you did great. I need you."

"You're crazy! You're insane, and I will never do another thing you ask for the rest of my life. Never."

Pete turned back to his cameraman. "He just needs a little time to get over the trauma . . . of running into a tree and all."

I tried to help Scott, but he didn't want to be touched. I did manage to pull the bike off of him.

In the meantime, Valerie had finished her rewrite. "Here you go. I rewrote that scene. You wanna hear it?"

"Sure," Pete said, undoubtedly hoping it wouldn't be as good as his draft.

Valerie cleared her throat and read from the new script, "'Rock, ever since I met you . . . garbage smells more disgusting . . . all men, other than you, seem more handsome . . . and muscles seem to be flabbier . . .'"

"All right, very funny," Pete said. "But this is not a comedy."

"There's where you're wrong, Pete. This *is* a comedy. This is the most hilarious thing I've ever been a part of. I look at this script and I cannot help but laugh my head off."

This went on for several minutes until Nelson came running up to me with a piece of paper. "Look at this." He handed me the paper and I quickly scanned it. "I'm being sued. For 100 starbills."

"One hundred starbills?!"

"Ryan, if I lose this case . . . I'm ruined."

SEVEN

THE TRIAL OF THE CENTURY

ONE HUNDRED STARBILLS WAS RIDICULOUS. There was no way that Nelson's "crime" was worth 100 starbills. That amount would ruin anyone.

Nelson tried to get his sister, Valerie, to represent him, but she was busy shooting the movie. Unfortunately, she was the best lawyer in town. The only other lawyer in town was Pete, who was also shooting the movie. So Nelson decided to be his own lawyer. No one had any idea who was going to represent Jake, the "victim."

We found five people to be on the jury. None of them had seen the accident and four of them didn't even know Jake, so they seemed impartial.

• • •

The meeting hall was packed. Almost everyone who wasn't involved with the movie shoot was there. Before taking my seat, I stopped by Nelson's table. "Keep your head up. You can trust the judgment of the people of this town."

"Will you testify for me?" he asked.

"Of course."

Jake made a dramatic entrance into the courtroom. He was on crutches and had a splint on his leg. He groaned just loud enough for everyone to hear him and asked several members of the audience for assistance. I saw Nelson bury his head in his hands. But as bad as Jake's appearance was, things were about to get worse. Right behind Jake, to the horror of everyone there, was the person who was to be his lawyer—Max Darby. A gasp echoed under the roof as they came in together. The loudest gasp came from Nelson.

I didn't think Max's presence was so bad, though. Max was smart and he was mean, and that made him the tougher lawyer. But everyone knew Max was dishonest and cruel. I hoped the jury would keep his reputation in mind. Many of the jurors themselves had probably been swindled by Max at some point. But there was no telling what Max would say to tear down Nelson's character. Win or lose, Nelson would be hurt by this trial.

Judge Amy called court into session. Nelson was sitting alone at a table in the front. Max moved their table so that Jake could stick his leg out far enough for the jury to see the splint. When the jury entered, that was the first thing they all saw.

The judge asked Jake to tell everyone, in his own words, what happened. Jake told the whole story. He was walking home when the car came out of nowhere and he stepped on it. He fell down and pulled a ligament in his ankle. The judge asked how he knew it was ligament damage. Max submitted a copy of a real doctor's report. It stated that Jake should stay off his feet because he had pulled a ligament in his ankle. The judge had the jury pass the slip of paper around, and then moved on.

Judge Amy asked how much money the plaintiff (Jake) was asking for. Max told her that since the injury had prevented Jake from doing his job (he mowed lawns), Nelson should pay him 100 starbills for lost wages.

"One hundred starbills seems like a lot of money, Mr. Darby," the judge said.

"Yes, Your Honor," Max said in the over-dramatized Southern accent he saved for really important swindles. "But since my client is losing real wages, that is, real money from the real world, we thought 100 starbills, which is, well . . . pretend money . . . would be about the right amount."

Judge Amy nodded her head, and then asked Nelson to begin. Nelson pleaded his case, telling everyone that he never had any intention to do anyone harm, and that it was a freak accident. Then he pointed out that if this had been a real car accident, it would be the fault of the driver, not the manufacturer of the car. I saw a juror nod, so I thought Nelson had made a good point.

Then Nelson called me to the stand. I talked about how I had been friends with Nelson for many years and that I would vouch for his good character. I told the jury that I believed he had only good intentions when he built those cars and that his business had been good for the city. Nelson smiled at me, and then told the judge he had no more questions for me.

I started to go back to my seat when Max suddenly said,

"I'd like to cross-examine the witness." What was he going to ask me?

I sat back down in the witness stand and nervously pushed my hair back off my forehead. Max stood up and approached me.

"Mr. Mayor, how long have you known Nelson Swanson?"

"About four years."

"And from what you've seen, what does he do with most of his time?"

"Well . . . he's always building things or coming up with new ideas . . ."

"So, he's an inventor?"

"Yes."

"I declare. Quite a noble profession," he said. "Besides the cars, what else has Nelson invented?"

"Um . . . lots of things. He made a burglar alarm, um . . . an air hockey table, an automatic soccer ball kicker—so goalies could practice keeping goal."

"Go on."

"Well, a couple of smaller things . . . a self-heating frying pan . . ."

"Self-heating frying pan? Now that sounds interesting."

"Yeah, he made it for Sid so he could sell egg and cheese sandwiches in the bakery."

"Mmm. Sounds good."

"It was battery-operated. You didn't need a stove."

"A marvel of technology. Tell me, how long did it take Nelson to make it?"

"I'm not sure. Maybe two months or so."

"Why'd it take so long?"

"He's kind of a perfectionist. It had to be perfect."

"But what was wrong with the first model?"

"The first model?"

"The very first time he tried this self-heating frying pan, did it not work?"

"I guess . . . not the very *first* time."

"What was wrong with it?"

I had no idea where he was going with this, but I figured I should tell the truth as I knew it to be. "I don't know. He could tell you better than I can."

"What happened when he first tried it out?"

I thought about it a second, then I remembered. Suddenly, I knew exactly where Max was going with this. I didn't see how I could avoid admitting something that would be damaging to Nelson's case. I decided to stall. "It . . . didn't work perfectly."

"What makes you say that?"

"The, um . . . wiring was a little off . . ."

"And what happened as a result of the bad wiring?"

"It . . . malfunctioned."

"How?"

"By . . . not working correctly."

He was getting impatient. "Mr. Mayor, isn't it true that the frying pan caught on *fire* in his house?"

"I seem to recall—"

"Mr. Mayor, you are under oath! Did it catch on fire?"

"It was just a small fire . . . and we put it out with an extinguisher."

"Nelson has a fire extinguisher in his house?"

"Yes."

"So apparently this happens to Nelson a lot, huh?"

"I wouldn't say that—"

"Wouldn't you agree that a person who has a fire extinguisher in his house does so because there might be a fire?"

"Oh, come on, Max—"

"Let's go back to the soccer ball kicker. Isn't it true, Mr. Mayor, that the first version of this invention nearly kicked Scott Sanchez's kneecap off?"

"It wasn't that bad."

"Did Scott Sanchez have to go to the doctor because of it?"

"It was Scott's fault—"

He started shouting. "Did Scott Sanchez have to have medical treatment done to his knee because of an invention that Nelson Swanson created, or not?"

He had me. I had no choice. "Yes."

"So, Mr. Mayor, is it fair to say that Nelson Swanson has a history of creating dangerous products?"

Nelson shouted from his chair, "Objection!"

"No further questions, Your Honor," Max said before the judge could answer the objection. All he wanted to do was get the jury thinking that Nelson was dangerous. And he was probably doing a good job of it. I stepped down and gave Nelson an "I'm sorry" look. He didn't respond because he appeared to be thinking up a new strategy.

"Nelson, do you have any more witnesses?" the judge asked.

"Yes," Nelson said. Nelson called a boy named Charlie to the witness stand.

"Charlie, is this your remote-controlled car?" Nelson held up the car that Jake had tripped on. It still had a crushed windshield.

"Yes."

"Were you operating the car on the day that Jake tripped on it?"

"No."

"What were you doing?"

"I was working on the movie shoot all day—holding a microphone."

"So, Charlie, did you loan your car to anyone?"

"No."

"Did you pre-program the car to operate at that specific time of day?"

"No."

"So, who was controlling the car?"

"I don't know."

"Did any of your friends have access to the car?"

"Not that I know of."

"Do you think someone stole your car?"

"Yes, I do."

"Isn't it a possibility that someone might've stolen your car, used it to stage a fake fall in order to sue—"

Max exploded out of his chair. "Objection! He's leading the witness."

"Sustained," Judge Amy said without hesitation.

"No more questions, Your Honor." Brilliant. Just as Max had done minutes earlier, Nelson had planted a seed of doubt in the jury's minds. Was all of this some kind of hoax? No one knew who had been operating the car. Surely this missing bit of information was crucial.

Max had no questions for Charlie, so Nelson continued. "I would like to call Eugene Meltsner to the stand."

Max objected to Nelson calling an adult, stating that because this was a kids' town, adults had no business interfering in the affairs of Kidsboro. Judge Amy overruled him, since one of his pieces of evidence, the doctor's slip, was signed by an adult. Amy was a fine judge.

Eugene stepped to the stand. Reverend Joey was working as the bailiff. He asked Eugene, "Do you promise to tell the truth, the whole truth, and nothing but the truth?"

"Indeed I do," he replied.

Nelson said, "Mr. Meltsner, you helped me build those cars. In your expert opinion, is there anything unsafe about them?"

"Undoubtedly, there are dangers inherent in any man-made mechanism, but I would consider these to be slight in the models created by Nelson Motors."

Confused silence settled upon the audience. Nelson noticed. "And that means?"

"No."

Eugene's testimony went on endlessly, somehow transforming every one-sentence answer into a four- or five-sentence answer. Finally, he was finished.

"The defense rests for now," Nelson said.

"All right, then. Max, do you have any witnesses?" Judge Amy inquired.

"I do, Your Honor." He called Nelson to the stand and asked him one question. "How much money did you make this summer, Mr. Swanson?" Nelson immediately objected, but for some reason, Judge Amy allowed it.

"About 125 starbills. But most of that went back into my company."

"No further questions." I couldn't believe Judge Amy would allow a ploy to get the jury to think, "Let's get the rich guy." It was a despicable strategy on Max's part, but it would probably work.

Max then called Jake to the stand. "Do you know Nelson Swanson, Mr. Randall?"

"Not really. I've met him. I know he's the one who built the car."

"Do you know Jill Segler?"

"I met her once. She interviewed me."

"How about Scott Sanchez?"

"Again, I met him once." Where was he going with this?

"Alice Funderburk."

"Cop, right?"

"That's right. Do you know her very well?"

"Nope."

"How about Mayor Ryan Cummings? Do you know him very well?"

Jake looked over at me with an evil smile. "Oh, yes. I know Ryan."

Nelson objected, "Your Honor, I fail to see the relevance—"

"Thank you, Mr. Randall. That's all," Max said.

Jake stepped down. Then Max pulled another unexpected move. "I'd like to call Ryan Cummings back up to the stand."

I looked at the judge, desperately hoping this was against the rules. But it wasn't. I slowly left my seat and took my place on the stand.

"Mr. Mayor, welcome back," Max said with a smile.

"Thanks," I said, rolling my eyes.

"Mr. Mayor, do you know Jake Randall?" Oh no. He wouldn't. Jake had probably told him something, and now Max was going to blackmail me. Or maybe it was something else. Maybe Max was just trying to scare me. I had to stay calm. If I acted nervous, or if I refused to answer the question, everyone in Kidsboro would know something was up. They'd all be asking me questions. I couldn't deal with that. I had to remain calm.

"Yes," I said.

"How well do you know him?"

"Not that well, really."

"Is he your friend?"

"I don't know if I would call him that. He's an acquaintance."

"Isn't he a little more than that?"

I gulped. "What do you mean?"

"He's a citizen of this town, isn't he?"

"Yes," I said, fearing a bad question was just around the corner. I shifted in my chair.

"It's very strange that he became a citizen. You know why? Because our city charter states that 80 percent of the city council has to approve a new citizen. That means four out of the five members of the city council had to vote for him. And yet . . . Jake just testified that he doesn't even know four out of the five members of the city council. He does, however, know you. Mr. Mayor, if Jake only knows one out of five people on the city council, could you tell us how it is that he became a citizen?"

I glanced over at Jake. He was trying to hide a smile.

"You must've recommended him very highly if they were convinced without ever meeting him."

I didn't answer.

"He must be a very good friend, Mr. Mayor. And we all know how much pride you take in your citizens. We all know you would never want a dishonest, untrustworthy person within the walls of Kidsboro. So, Mr. Mayor, when Jake says that these events took place . . . you know, with the car and all . . . you believe him, don't you?"

He had me again. I couldn't question Jake's character. I took a deep breath and prepared to lie. "If that's what he said . . . I guess it happened."

"And do you think Jake would ever be a part of any hoax, Mr. Mayor?"

"I . . . suppose not."

"Thank you, Mr. Mayor." Thankfully, I got to get off the

stand. My heart was pumping against my chest like a bongo drum.

"No further questions," Max said. "We rest our case, Your Honor."

The judge allowed each lawyer to restate his case. Nelson's sounded pretty flimsy up against Max's, I must say. I couldn't quite read the jury's faces. I just hoped they remembered the other scams that Max had pulled in the past. That was probably Nelson's only hope. The jury left to discuss the verdict.

• • •

Nelson remained in his chair behind the table. I wanted to say I was sorry, but I didn't think it would matter at this point. I would wait until the verdict was in.

I decided to get out of there before anyone asked me any questions about Jake. On my way out, I ran into him. He was maneuvering himself out from under the pavilion roof on his crutches. He smiled and patted me on the back. "Thanks for saying such nice things about me, Ryan."

Fuming, I grabbed him by the arm and led him away from the crowd. "What are you guys doing?" I demanded once we were out of earshot.

"Who?"

"You and Max."

"We're tryin' to win a case."

"What did you tell him?"

"About what?"

"You know about what," I said, fisting the bottom of his shirt up into a wad.

"Man, you're really scared of me." I let go of his shirt. I was giving myself away. "I didn't tell him nothing. Don't worry." He headed back to the meeting hall. "We're pals, remember?"

I watched him walk away. I didn't want to be scared of him. But I was.

• • •

The jury would probably be out for a while, so I decided to take a break from reality and check out Kidsboro's version of Hollywood. The movie shoot had been in progress for over a week now. The last time I had been there, things weren't going terribly well. I hoped Pete had been able to smooth some things over.

When I got there, Pete was filming at the bottom of the cliff and had apparently just finished a scene. Scott was lying at the base of the cliff, moaning. Lying next to him were three garbage bags filled with couch cushions. The bags were painted to look like rocks. From the looks of things, Scott had just been asked to stand under a cliff while rocks landed on top of him. I guess Pete had misjudged the weight of the couch cushions, because Scott looked to be in quite a daze. He was mumbling something about naptime.

Then Valerie stormed up with a piece of paper in her hand. She went straight to Pete and stuck her finger in his face. Everyone else on the crew stopped what they were doing and filed in behind her. Pete watched them, clueless.

"Mr. Director, the entire cast and crew met last night after we were done taping. We met to discuss how we were feeling about this movie production. As it turns out, Pete, everyone felt pretty much the same way. We're all sick of you!"

"What?"

"You've pushed us way too hard. We're 10 to 14 years old. We shouldn't have to work 60-hour weeks."

"I thought you *liked* doing this," Pete said.

"We *used* to like doing this. But you've completely taken the fun out of it for everyone."

"How?"

"Funny you should ask that. At the meeting last night, we came up with a list of grievances. And from that, a list of demands. We will refuse to work until every last one of these demands is met."

"Refuse to work? You can't do that. You're under contract."

"We're breaking it, unless these demands are met."

"Okay, what demands?"

Valerie cleared her throat and read aloud, "We will get a one-hour lunch break every day."

"All right, I can deal with that," Pete said.

"We will not work past seven o'clock in the evening, unless we are given overtime pay."

"I suppose I could work around the seven o'clock thing. But you're not getting overtime. We're over budget as it is."

Valerie went on. "The cast and crew will be allowed to have as much creative input as they desire."

"What do you mean by that?"

"We can change the script if we want to."

"No way. This is *my* film—"

She ignored him and went back to the list. "The actors

will not be required to touch other actors." I was certain this one was Valerie's demand.

"What? You've gotta be kidding! The script has to have—"

"We will not be required to travel over 15 miles an hour and run into solid objects, and we will not be required to have solid objects that are traveling over 15 miles an hour run into *us*." Scott's demand, obviously.

"This is ridiculous."

"We will not be required to do any more method-acting exercises where we have to act like we're a kitchen appliance for an entire day." I could understand this one. Scott was clearly embarrassed one day when he had wrecked trying to ride a bicycle like a toaster oven.

"What gives you guys the right to question my techniques? *I'm* the artist here. Spielberg doesn't have to answer to his actors."

"You're not Spielberg. And you'll give us what we want or we walk."

"No way. I can deal with some of those things, but I can't turn my set into a free-for-all. I have to have control."

"Fine. Then we're officially on strike."

"You can't be serious!"

"Come on, everybody." Valerie dropped the list on the ground in front of Pete. The group filed away quietly. Scott got up from the bottom of the cliff and followed.

"*Nobody's* staying? Oh, come on!" Pete picked up the list. "I'll give you the lunch break . . . and the quitting at seven o'clock deal! Except for night shoots, of course. Okay, no more method-acting exercises! I'll give you that one." Pete continued to yell out at them, but no one even turned around. Pete suddenly turned defiant. "You'll be back! You need this job! A lot of you don't even *have* other jobs! And you know what? I can finish this movie without you!"

I turned to Pete and shrugged my shoulders. "Maybe a little compromise wouldn't hurt."

"Compromise is what makes bad movies," he said, turning and putting his equipment away.

• • •

I got back to the meeting hall just in time. The jury was in place and ready to read the verdict. I sat down and glanced at Nelson. He was fidgeting in his seat. A juror handed a piece of paper to the judge and she read it.

"Has the jury reached a verdict?" she asked.

The foreman of the jury stood up. "Yes, Your Honor."

"Go ahead."

"We, the jury, find for the plaintiff." Nelson had lost. A gasp went through the crowd and Nelson's head practically dropped to the floor. The foreman went on, "For the entire 100 starbills." Another gasp. Nelson's head bent even further down. I looked around. One person knocked over a chair in anger; another pounded his fist into a post. They were both investors in Nelson's company. All that money they had invested was gone. Another boy shouted "No!" and buried his head in his hands. It was one of Nelson's employees. He was probably out of a job. Until this moment, I hadn't realized just how many people this lawsuit would affect. Max and Jake were giving each other high-fives, and they left the room taunting Nelson. Nelson continued to sit there and stare at the ground. I went over to him.

"I'm finished," he said.

"You can rebuild," I told him. "You've got a good product."

"How am I gonna get any investors after this? I can't build cars anymore. I'm done."

• • •

A week after the verdict, our two biggest industries were gone. Nelson Motors was bankrupt, and Pete's movie was on hold because of the strike. Investors in both were furious. All of Nelson's employees had to be laid off. Also, some of the investors had their own businesses, and when they lost the money they had put into Nelson Motors, some of *their* employees had to be laid off too. In short, no one in Kidsboro (except for Max and Jake) had any money. And because no one had any money, that meant that no one had any money to spend—so businesses were failing. No one was playing miniature golf anymore or going to the movies. Unemployment was growing and it showed no signs of getting any better.

But it could get worse.

EIGHT

THE GREAT DEPRESSION

MARCY CAME TO MY OFFICE after she was done at the bank for the day. She looked rattled. "Ryan, can I talk to you for a minute?"

"Sure." I motioned for her to come in. She sat down and hit my desk with her knee, almost knocking over a clock.

"Sorry."

"That's okay." Her face paled. I felt sorry for her and I didn't even know what was the matter yet.

"We've got a problem. The bank is almost out of money."

"What?"

"You see . . . everybody's broke, and so people are taking their money out of the bank because they suddenly need it. And the people who took out loans to start their new businesses, well . . . they can't pay their loans back because they don't have any customers anymore."

"So, there's all sorts of money going *out* of the bank, but no money coming *in*?"

"Exactly."

"Oh, boy."

"We wouldn't be so low except that Max withdrew all of his money—212 starbills."

"Why did Max take out his money?"

"He said he had some things to buy."

"With 212 starbills? There's nothing in Kidsboro that costs that much."

"I didn't ask him about that. I didn't think it was any of my business."

"Oh, man. This is bad. If this gets out, everybody's going to want to get their money out of the bank as soon as possible," I said. "And if the money runs out, a lot of people are gonna be really angry."

"I know. Some people put everything they owned in the bank."

To be honest, I was tempted to take out my own money. I had almost 20 starbills in that bank and I couldn't afford to lose it. But I couldn't do that to Marcy or to Kidsboro.

"How much do we have left?"

"Twenty-three starbills. And some change."

"Okay." I got up and began to pace around. I had to think. "Okay . . . if anybody wants to take out any money tomorrow, try to convince them not to. Make up any reason."

"I could raise interest rates."

"Yes. Good. Tell them that for this week, and this week only, the interest rate is raised three percentage points. They could earn extra money for keeping it in there for one more week. Figure out exactly how much and tell them."

"Okay."

"And get on these guys who owe the bank money."

"I've already talked to them. No one has anything to pay back."

"I'll go out tomorrow and bring Alice with me. She'll squeeze it out of them."

"Oh, yeah. That might work."

"And most importantly, Marcy . . . don't tell *anyone* about this. Not your best friend, not your mother, not even your teddy bear."

"I won't."

"If this gets out, we're *all* in deep trouble."

• • •

The next day I asked Alice to help me collect some debts. I knocked on doors and asked people to please pay back the money they owed the bank. Most said they didn't have any money, until Alice stepped inside and threatened to turn them upside down by their ankles. Then they suddenly remembered that they *did* have a little money stashed away somewhere. The plan worked. We were able to retrieve 19 starbills, but that wasn't nearly as much as what was owed. People genuinely had no money, and no amount of being turned upside down could get them to pay up. By the end of the day, I was happy with what we got. I was pretty sure that the 19 starbills we had collected, plus the 23 already in the bank, would hold us for another few days.

• • •

I was surprised to see Pete with a camera. He was apparently getting ready to film a scene. I walked over, but didn't see any of the regular actors or crew around. It was just Pete and his six-year-old sister, Robin. Robin was sitting at a table facing someone I didn't recognize at first. The face was turned away from me. Maybe Pete was filming something for his family.

"What are you doing, Pete?"

"Making my film."

"What film?"

"The film I've been making for the last few weeks," he said matter-of-factly, as though it was a stupid question.

"I didn't know your sister was in it."

"She is now."

"What role is she playing?"

"Right now she's Ginger." He looked through his viewfinder and dollied the camera a little to his left.

"What do you mean?"

"I told them I could make this film without them. And I will."

"How is Robin going to play Ginger?"

"Robin's a very talented actress. You'd be surprised."

"So, you're just going to throw out all the stuff you filmed with Valerie as Ginger?"

"Nope. I'm keeping it." This was getting tiresome. I wished he would just tell me what was going on.

"How are you going to explain how Ginger suddenly changed from a 14 year old with long, brown hair into a six year old with curly, black hair?"

"With this." Pete held up a plain silver mask, which he took over to Robin. "Here. You can put this on now." She tied it around her head and he came back and looked through the viewfinder. He glanced toward me. "I changed the script a little bit. Now, Ginger has some kind of dental surgery and has to wear this mask for a month."

"So, she's going to wear this thing for the rest of the movie?"

"Yep. You see, it makes perfect sense, because if you'll remember, earlier in the film Ginger talks about being engaged to a dentist."

"So?"

"Well, it's natural to assume that her fiancé would recognize her need for surgery. It's perfectly logical."

"Oh, right," I said.

He looked back toward Robin. "Pull the mask a little toward your right ear."

"Who's that?" I asked, pointing to whoever was sitting in the chair opposite her. I still hadn't seen his face, and he hadn't moved an inch since I got there.

"That's the bad guy."

I walked around where I could see the bad guy's face, and as soon as I saw it, I almost burst out laughing. "A giant teddy bear?"

"All you can see is the back of his clothes. When I change angles, *I'll* play the bad guy."

"With a dental surgery mask on?"

"No. I'll just duck behind flowers and stuff. Wear a hat."

I raised my eyebrows.

"It'll work," Pete insisted.

"No, it *won't* work," came a voice from behind me. Pete and I whirled around and saw Mark, the owner and creator of the miniature golf place. His face was red.

Pete ignored Mark and continued to work.

"You're not going to do this, Pete!"

"Go away, Mark."

"I invested a lot of money in this movie, and you've got your six-year-old sister playing the romantic lead? I don't think so."

"I've got it all figured out. You'll never know the difference."

"Listen to me, Pete." Pete continued to look through the viewfinder.

Mark walked around in front of the camera and spoke into the lens. "Listen to me. I've got a business to run. I've got loans that I can't pay back. This movie needs to be made, and it needs to be made *now*. You will give the actors *everything* they want."

"I can't do that."

"You have to."

"If I give in now, they'll just want more and more."

"I don't care."

"This is my movie!"

"But it's my money you're making this movie *with*!"

"Investors have no say in how a movie is produced."

"I don't know where you're getting all these rules. But you'd better close your little rule book and start negotiating with the actors. Now." Mark pushed on the side of the camera, rolling it to the edge of the flat, wood piece it was sitting on. He took one last angry look at Pete and left. Pete hesitated only a second, then moved his camera back into place.

"You know, Pete, he's probably right," I said.

"Would you mind leaving the set, Ryan? I'm trying to concentrate."

I turned on my heel and left.

• • •

Scott ran up to me, grabbed my arm, and pulled me behind a tree. He looked around to see if anyone was nearby.

"What is it?"

Scott came close and whispered, "You need to go to the bank."

"Why?"

"It's almost out of money."

I suddenly lost feeling in my lips. "How do you know that?"

"A bunch of people are talking about it. I just withdrew everything I had in there. You'd better do the same before it—"

Before he could finish his sentence, I was sprinting toward the bank.

I could hear people yelling before I could even see the bank. When I finally saw it, I came to a complete stop. There was a crowd of people outside the door, demanding to get in. A "Closed" sign hung on the door and Marcy was desperately trying to keep people out. I went to try to make peace, knowing full well I had nothing to tell them that would make anyone feel better.

Valerie was the first to see me, and she ran over to me. "Is this true? Is all our money just . . . gone?"

"Look, Valerie . . ." A couple of people saw us talking and filtered over to me. "There's not much I can do."

"This was your idea, Cummings!" Valerie shouted into my face. "This whole bank thing was your brilliance at work. Now you've got 20 people here who are completely broke!"

"Listen . . . some people are having trouble paying off their loans. As soon as we get that money, we'll be able to give you everything you put in."

"And how are these people going to pay off their loans? They're probably broke too. Right?" I was hoping that nobody would be able to think two steps ahead. I shouldn't have underestimated Valerie.

"I—" I stuttered. "I'll work this out. I just need to talk to Marcy."

"You'd *better* work it out, Cummings! And you'd better do it fast or you'll pay for this." Valerie yelled at me as I moved past her.

I made my way through the crowd. A few people bumped me and a few more said some harsh things to me. I called out to Marcy to open the door. She unlocked it. I pried the door open against the weight of a couple of people leaning on it. I pushed them out of the way, slammed the door, and locked it behind me. Marcy was leaning against the back wall, petrified.

The noise outside was muffled, but still loud. I had to raise my voice for her to hear me.

"What happened? I thought we were going to keep this quiet."

"I didn't tell anyone. I was gonna yell at *you* for telling somebody."

"I didn't tell a soul."

"Then how . . ." she started, but faded.

"Is there any money left at all?"

"Forty-seven tokens."

"Where do you keep the money?"

"In a safe down here. I take it home with me every night. And I'm the only one who knows the combination."

"Let me see your laptop."

"Here."

"Show me how to find out how much money is left."

She punched a few keys, and I looked at the screen.

"Was there any time today when you left this laptop alone?"

"No. I was in here all day."

"How about yesterday?"

"No."

"You never took a break, you never ran an errand? Nothing?"

She thought for a second. "No, I . . . wait a minute. Yes, I guess I did leave it, but it was only for a minute or so."

"What were you doing?"

"I went to help somebody put up a street sign. He needed me to hold it while he—"

"A street sign?"

"Yeah, it was a yield sign. I didn't really understand why we needed one there, but this guy was putting it up."

"Who was it?"

"I don't remember his name, but it was that guy who sued Nelson."

"Jake?"

"Yeah, Jake. That's who it was."

I gritted my teeth. There was something going on here. Someone was trying to destroy the town, and I had a good idea who it was. The only problem was that I had no proof.

• • •

I remembered in history class when we learned about the Great Depression, which occurred in the United States in the 1920s and 1930s. The banks ran out of money and people lost all their savings. Unemployment was very high, so no one had any money to pay for anything. Businesses failed everywhere. If it was anything like what was happening in Kidsboro, the Great Depression was named well. A dreariness seemed to hang over the city like heavy fog. Half the citizens of Kidsboro lost their savings when the bank went under. A third got fired from their jobs. No one was buying anything; no one was selling anything. I didn't catch very many people even smiling anymore. A once-proud city was now just a couple of steps away from being a ghost town.

NINE

THE INVESTIGATION

THE ONLY WAY I COULD see us getting out of this depression was to figure out how to prove that Jake's accident was a hoax. I got to work immediately.

I needed to find some place where those guys had slipped up. Something about their testimony in court that didn't make sense. Something that couldn't have possibly happened.

The first place I looked was the newspaper office. I asked Jill to show me the article that she ran about the accident. I knew there was an interview with Jake in there. I also asked to see the article about the trial. I took them both out and laid them side by side on the table, searching for something . . . anything.

As I flipped through the pages, Jill came over. "What are you looking for?"

"I don't know yet," I said.

Then I found it. "Look at this. Right here. Jake changed his story. In his interview with you after the accident, he said he was walking toward the *bakery* when the accident occurred. During the trial, he told everyone that he was going to the *movie shoot*. From where he was standing, that's going in two different directions!"

"Are you sure?"

"Here." I grabbed a piece of paper and a pen and quickly drew a rough sketch of the town. "If he was walking toward the bakery," I drew a dotted line to show the direction Jake was moving, "at that angle, if he went as far as he could go, he'd end up in the creek. The movie shoot was all the way over here." I drew a circle to indicate where the filming was taking place.

"But how do you know he was walking from *here*?" Jill said, pointing to the spot where I'd written "Jake."

"Well . . . didn't he say that?"

"No. He never said where he was before the accident. He only said which direction he was going in."

"But he said two different things. To you, he said he was going to the bakery. In court, he said he was going to the movie shoot."

"No, he told me he was going *toward* the bakery. That's just a *direction*. Going to the movie shoot means he was actually headed there—in *whatever* direction." She was right. I looked down at the map and tried to figure out why she was wrong. But she wasn't.

"What's going on?" she asked.

"Huh?" I replied.

"Why are you doing this?"

"I guess I'm just frustrated with the verdict."

"Do you really think Jake made it all up?"

"I . . . don't know."

"What have you heard? What makes you think he's lying?"

I looked her straight in the face. I knew I could trust Jill, even more than Scott. I couldn't tell her everything, but I had to get my town back. "I just think he is," I told her.

"Why? Did he say something? Look at you in some weird way? What?"

"I just have this feeling . . ."

"That's not good enough!" she suddenly lashed out. I jumped. "What's going on with you, Ryan?"

"What do you mean?"

"What do I mean? You call a city council meeting to nominate Jake to be a citizen. We've never heard of the guy, yet you tell us he could be a real asset to our community. None of us really goes for it, so you ask us to trust you. So we do. We vote him in. I figure he's got to be a great guy if you nominated him, but you never introduce him to any of us. I never even see you *with* him. And now, you're telling me you think he's lying. But you have no reason to believe that. You just think he's lying. Now tell me the truth, Ryan. Is this guy a real asset to our community or is he a liar?" She was standing with her face six inches from mine, glaring into my eyes.

"He's a liar."

"Then why did you make him a citizen?"

"Jill . . ." I pulled out a chair and sat down. I didn't know what to do next. She closed her eyes and knelt down next to me.

"Are you in trouble?" she asked. "Because I've never

known you to lie to anybody, much less your friends . . . so something must be seriously wrong here. Did he threaten to beat you up?"

"No."

"Cause if he did, you know you've got Alice."

"He didn't threaten to beat me up."

"Then what?" I turned away from her. She grabbed my chair and turned it forcefully around so that I was looking right at her.

"Ryan . . ." she said quietly. "I'm your friend. And when you ask me to trust you, I do. Every time. You've never given me any reason not to trust you. But now you need to trust *me*." She took my hand between both of hers and held it tightly. I was completely comfortable with her. I always had been, since the day I met her. I had no trouble trusting her with my secret, but this wasn't about trust. It was about putting her in danger. They had told us at the shelter that telling who we were would not only put us in danger, it would put everyone we told in danger too.

"Okay. I can't tell you exactly what's going on because . . . well, I just can't. But I will tell you that he's threatened me with something and I think he's trying to sabotage the city."

"Why?"

"Because of something I did to him a long time ago. He wants to get me back."

She smiled slightly. "Okay. That's a good start. At some point I'd like to know the whole story, but I understand if you don't want to tell me everything. Now . . . what do you want me to do?"

"I'm looking for proof that Jake—and maybe Max—staged the accident in order to win all that money."

I told her the whole story about how Max had taken all his money out of the bank, then sometime afterward, Marcy had gone to help Jake put up a street sign—possibly so Max could get in the bank and look at the computer files. Jill thought it sounded fishy too.

We spent the afternoon in my office, looking through the articles and photos from the crime scene and the trial. One picture caught my eye. I couldn't quite put my finger on it, but something was wrong. It was a picture of the damaged car. I snatched the Kidsboro map off the table and laid it alongside the picture. Jill peered over my shoulder. Suddenly it hit me.

"I've got it. Okay, the car was coming from *this* way, right?" I said, making a straight line with my finger on the map.

"Right."

"And Jake was walking this way."

"Right."

"So look at the way the car is crushed. You can plainly see the shape of a foot."

"Yes."

"But it's backwards. If he ran into it head-on, the heel should've landed on the front of the hood, right?"

"I see where you're going," Jill said. "This car is crushed like Jake came up from *behind* it."

"Exactly. And look at how much the car has been damaged. If the car simply tripped him, Jake would've fallen off quickly and his full weight never would've been on top of the car . . ."

"But this looks like somebody just stomped on it."

"That's it. You think this'll hold up in court?" I asked.

"Not a chance. The car could've made a sharp turn right when it came up on Jake, plus he could've turned his body. But this is a start. We need more evidence."

The discovery had given us our second wind. We were onto something, and nothing could stop us now. We hurried back to the newspaper office.

"Listen, Jill." I stopped. "If we do find something, and we take this back to court . . . you have to do it. Jake can't know that I had anything to do with this."

"Gotcha. I'll do it."

• • •

Late that afternoon, we decided to take a look at the crushed car. We checked first at the police station, because we figured since it had been evidence for the trial, Alice would have it. But Alice told us that she had given it back to Nelson once the trial was over, because he wanted to put it back together. So we walked to Nelson's, hoping he hadn't begun repairing it.

When we got there, we were shocked to discover that Nelson Motors was up and running again. Nelson was inside with his designer, looking at a picture of what would be their next model. Jill and I exchanged confused looks. "What's going on?" I asked.

Nelson glanced up at us, then motioned for us to follow him outside. We did. "Someone donated some money to us,"

Nelson said. "We're back. We've got eight more cars to build, and I think I can pay off the investors and my employees with the profits."

"Who donated the money?"

Nelson looked at the ground and spread some dirt around with his foot. He said quietly, "Max."

I gave him a stern look. "I know, I know," he said. "It's probably a mistake. But what else was I going to do? I've got people all over the place who want their money back. I have a responsibility to them. Sure, I'll probably have to be Max's slave for a while . . . but at least I'll be able to pay off my debts."

I didn't like the sound of that arrangement. We asked about the car. Nelson had already begun repairing it, so it was useless to look at it.

On our way back to the newspaper office, we noticed someone on the miniature golf course. Mark was watching four people play a round together. There was a big sign on the office door that read, "GRAND REOPENING."

"You're open again?"

"Sure. You wanna play?"

"No thanks. We're on our way somewhere. I thought you had a lot of debts to pay."

"Max took care of it for me."

"Max?"

"Yeah, you know, I owed him most of the money anyway—for the wood to build this thing. But he told me to forget it. And get this: He even gave me some money to hire an employee since I have to go to swimming lessons in the mornings now."

Jill and I exchanged looks. This was not looking good.

"I gotta tell you. After the trial, I kind of thought that Max was a jerk, you know? But he saved me, man. He saved the whole town."

Max was now the town hero.

• • •

Within a week, all the businesses were back up and running. The bank was back too, since Max had paid off some of the loans that other people couldn't pay. Many people were able to get their savings back. Everywhere I went, people were singing Max's praises.

Max even gave Pete enough money to start filming again. With his investors breathing down his neck, and his sister Robin beginning to make demands of her own, Pete agreed to let the actors have everything they wanted. With everyone happy, Pete put Valerie and Kirk back in front of the camera.

• • •

That night, Pete opened up the movie theater with a special discount showing of *Rocky*. Twenty-four of Kidsboro's 31 citizens filed in. Pete introduced the movie as a celebration of the rebirth of Kidsboro. Several people clapped, but the applause was slow and halfhearted.

During the movie, the laughter seemed a little forced; the sarcastic comments from the crowd were not quite as sharp as usual. The inspirational scenes in the movie didn't make anyone sit up straight or bounce their knees.

It was almost as if everyone was scared to celebrate.

• • •

My fears began to be realized the next morning.

"What's with this muffin, Sid?" I asked. I almost always had a muffin at Sid's Bakery in the morning. This one was not up to his usual standards.

Sid rolled his eyes and lowered his voice. "I had to put extra cinnamon in it."

"What do you mean, you *had* to?"

"He likes cinnamon."

"Who?"

"Max, of course. He gave me a loan to start the business up again, so I kind of have to do what he wants. He told me to put more cinnamon in everything. So I did."

"You put more cinnamon in *everything*?" I asked.

"Yep."

"But he's not going to eat everything."

"Doesn't matter. He told me he was making a business decision. And as he said, people like cinnamon."

"But this doesn't taste as good as it usually does."

"No kidding," Sid said.

"Did you tell him that?"

"He's not an easy person to disagree with. I'm sure you've noticed that."

"Yes, I have."

Next, I stopped by the newspaper office to see if Jill had come up with anything else.

"I saw something today that made me a little curious," she said.

"What?"

"It may be nothing, but I saw Max and Barry together."

"What were they doing?"

"Just talking. They were on the other side of the creek, like it was some secret meeting."

"So?"

"I don't think they're friends. And they have nothing in common."

"Right."

"Except for the fact that Max was the lawyer for the trial, and Barry was on the jury."

"You think Max bought him off?"

"I can't prove it . . ."

"Jury tampering would be tough to prove. But I agree. That's really strange."

Jill sat down and bent her head over the mess of papers and photos she had scoured a thousand times before. "There's something we're missing," she said. "I know there's something obvious here, something that'll prove our case without a doubt—but I just can't put my finger on it."

"I know how you feel. I can sense it too."

We brainstormed a while longer, and then I went home to rest my weary brain.

• • •

I dodged one of Nelson's cars as I was coming back into town. As it passed me, it got stuck on a tree root. Its wheels turned furiously but without success. I was about to reach down and give it some assistance when I heard, "Don't touch it, Ryan." It was Nelson. He and an employee were standing 20 feet behind me. Nelson's arms hung limply at his sides as if he had lost all hope in whatever he was doing.

"It just doesn't work!" Nelson shouted. I had never seen one of Nelson's cars get stuck. I walked over and joined them.

"What's wrong?" I asked.

"The new cars don't work," Nelson said. "We usually put four-wheel drive into all our vehicles. It's a luxury, and if you're going to use it on the street, you don't need it. But when you're in the woods, you've got to get over tree roots, leaves, rocks, branches, grooves in the soil. These things just don't work out here without four-wheel drive."

"I don't understand."

"Max came in yesterday and started watching our operation. He noticed us putting in extra components and asked why. We told him about the four-wheel drive, and he said that the cars don't need it. He said he wants our company to start being more cost-effective, and since we're using his money, he gets to call the shots."

"Oh, boy," I said.

"I argued with him for about an hour, but he wouldn't have it any other way."

"Maybe you could show him that it doesn't work."

"He doesn't care. It makes no difference to him if we sell an inferior product. He just wants us to sell as many as we can as soon as possible. This company's always been known for quality. If we start selling people *this* stuff, what happens next year when I want to start making something else?"

"Maybe you could put in the four-wheel drive and he won't notice."

Nelson shook his head. "He's got a new rule. All cars have to get his approval before they go out to be sold."

"This is bad."

"What exactly am I supposed to do?"

• • •

We were to see much more of this as the days went on. Throughout the city, businesses that sold things now had "price scales," where friends of Max paid less for everything, while everyone else paid top dollar for the same things. For instance, Max's friends got to play a round of golf for five tokens, while *I* had to pay 10 tokens. I knew I needed to call a city council meeting to discuss a new law regarding this practice. This was discrimination or something. Even worse, the course was now called "Putt to the Max," in honor of its new financial backer. There was a huge sign right in front of the course.

But it was at an evening film shoot that things really came to a head. I was sitting on a lawn chair just close enough to the set to observe without being in the way. Pete was getting a scene ready when Max showed up with a script in his hand. "Okay, I've made some changes."

"What?" Pete said.

"I've just made a few small revisions on this scene. I think it works a whole lot better." Pete took the script from Max, gave him a nervous smile, then scanned the pages. His mouth immediately turned down, then his eyes widened in horror. He seemed to calm himself, and then looked back up at Max, faking a smile.

"You know, Max . . . I don't think we can do this."

"Why not?"

"This is . . . um . . . kind of disgusting, and there's some bad language in here."

"Yeah, I know. I thought the character of Ginger needed some more . . . umph. She was too flat."

Hearing her screen name, Valerie immediately wanted the scoop. "Wait a minute. What did you do to Ginger?" Valerie grabbed the script from Pete and started scanning it.

"Max," Pete said, "this is supposed to be a family film. I don't use that kind of language in my films."

"How do you know? You've only made one."

Valerie wasn't yet done reading the page, but she was already shaking her head and saying, "I'm not saying this . . . I'm not doing this . . . I'm definitely not saying *that* . . ."

"Listen to me," Max said. "This will make the movie seem more real. People use this kind of language in real life. You want this movie to be realistic, right?"

"Not if I have to embarrass myself and my family," Pete said.

"Your family? What's your family got to do with it?"

"I've been telling them all about how well this project is going, and they can't wait until they get to see it for the first time. I am *not* going to have them come here and hear that stuff coming out of anybody's mouth."

"No way, Max," Valerie added. "I'm not saying this stuff. Forget it."

"Oh, come on, Val. I've heard you say stuff your momma wouldn't be too proud of."

"Well, I'm not putting it on film," Pete said. "Now get outta here."

Max smiled his evil smile. "You guys don't get it, do you? *I'm* running the show here. Pete might be the director, but there's nothing going on without me. If you don't say what I want you to say, there's no movie."

"Fine. Then there's no movie," Valerie said. Pete snapped a look toward her.

"Wait, wait," Pete said. "Let's just take the script and talk about it for a second. I think we can come to some kind of agreement."

"I think we can too. And I think we'll do it my way."

"But Max . . ."

Max gave him a stern look. "We *will* do it my way."

There was a long pause. Everyone looked at Pete.

"I can't."

"All right," Max snapped. "Then I guess there's no movie." He looked around at the cast and crew. "None of you are getting paid anymore. Which pretty much means, that's a wrap, people! Everybody can go on home!" He left quickly.

Valerie and Pete looked at each other, then Valerie rolled her eyes and packed up her makeup and left. Pete and the rest of the crew soon followed.

• • •

A day later, we held a scheduled town meeting. Thirty of 31 people showed up. There was nothing on the agenda until

Max stood up to make a motion. I had no idea what he was going to suggest, and I was horrified when he finally uncovered his agenda. He wanted to officially change the name of the town to Maxboro. We had no laws regarding the name of the city, so legally he could bring it before the city and call for a vote. All he needed was a majority consensus. He stood up in front of the crowd and took the vote. All the people who owed him money raised their hands. The final vote was a reluctant 16 to 14 in favor of switching the name to Maxboro, but I could see that everyone was fed up with Max's changes.

I was determined to put this on the agenda in the upcoming city council meeting. We had to put a stop to this, but for now, the city was officially named Maxboro.

• • •

Our church had more people in it than I had ever seen there before. It was practically the only place in Kidsboro that wasn't run by Max, and this apparently appealed to a lot of us. I counted 15 people. I sat between Jill and Scott.

Joey had something to say today. He came out with fire in his eyes. Perhaps he had been inspired by one of his dad's sermons. Perhaps he had read something in the Bible. But more than likely, he had seen what was happening in Kidsboro—and he wanted to say something about it.

He slapped his Bible on the front cover and immediately had us turn to Joshua chapter seven. He told the story of Achan. Joshua commanded the Israelite troops, and he sent 3,000 men out to conquer this tiny little place (with a tiny little army) called Ai. The Israelites got there, and the 3,000 men were defeated. Joshua was shocked, and so he asked God, "Why did you let this happen?" God told him that because Israel had disobeyed Him, He let their army be defeated. Joshua didn't know what God was talking about, so he went back to his men and asked, "Who disobeyed God?" Finally, Achan confessed, saying that he had stolen some things from God.

"Can you believe this?" Joey said, and I could almost hear his father's voice coming out of him. "An entire army was destroyed because of one man!" Joey went on, and though he didn't use the most poetic language or organize his thoughts in the most effective way, he made an excellent point. "We have an effect on our society. Whether we know it or not, our actions affect others. We have a responsibility to live an honorable life—if not for ourselves, then for the benefit of others." I immediately thought of the lawsuit against Nelson, a selfish act that had ended up causing the entire town to go into a tailspin. One single act.

"Amen!" I heard from behind me. Mr. Whittaker was sitting in the back row, gleaming with pride at Joey's revelation.

Joey went on to tell the story of Jesus feeding the 5,000. "Jesus had no food to offer the people, so He asked around for help from the crowd. One boy came up with just five loaves of bread and two fish. Jesus took what the boy gave, and He performed a miracle, feeding all 5,000 with this little bit of food. Can you see how one small, *un*selfish, honorable act helped the whole crowd?"

Joey finished his spirited sermon, and I wanted to stand and cheer. We sang a hymn, took up an offering, and we all filed out. Before everyone left, I suggested that we get together on Monday and talk—the 15 of us, and anyone else who wanted to come. I wanted to tell them not to invite Max, but I thought that might be rude. Besides, I think that was understood.

• • •

On Monday, everyone still seemed to be energized by Joey's sermon. We'd all had some time to think things over, and I was hoping this meeting would generate some ideas. All 15 people showed up including, surprisingly, Valerie. Before we even started the meeting, Scott came through the door. "Um . . . " he said with a frown, "I think there's something we need to go see."

The entire group filed out, and Scott led us to the outskirts of the town. We stopped when we saw what Scott was pointing to. There, 30 feet in front of us, were Max and Jake pounding a sign into the ground that read: "Welcome to Maxboro." Underneath, in small letters, it said, "Land of Opportunity." My shoulders drooped. Jill's eyes were glazed over as though she was about to cry. Scott bit his lip. Nelson looked down at the ground with his hand on the back of his neck. Alice cracked her knuckles as if in preparation to hit something. We were completely silent as we all stared at this spectacle, wondering what had become of our city.

Finally, Kirk spoke up, "I'm gonna go home." A couple of others agreed and followed. They drifted toward their individual homes.

"Wait!" I said. They all stopped. "Hang on a second. I've

got an idea." I'd gotten everyone's attention, though they didn't look hopeful. "Why don't we make our movie?"

Pete shook his head. "Ryan, I don't have the money to pay anybody since I won't go along with Max's changes."

"I know, but . . . Kirk? Valerie? What do you say? You can work for free, can't you? Scott? The rest of you guys in the crew? I'll help out too." Everyone sort of stared at me blankly. "Come on, now. We need something to give us our town back."

Scott looked around, and when no one else volunteered, he said, "All right, Pete, I'll be your stuntman for free."

"Thanks, Scott," I said. "Anybody else?"

"I'll do it," Kirk joined in.

"Yeah, me too," Valerie said. Soon, everyone in the cast and crew had agreed to work for free in order to finish the movie.

Pete got a sudden burst of energy and shouted, "All right!" and pumped his fist in the air.

"All right!" I repeated, and suddenly everyone forgot about going home. Instead, they went straight to the movie set. Maybe with this one unselfish act, we could get our town back.

• • •

That first day of filming again was extraordinary, almost magical. Pete was sharp and creative, while Valerie and Kirk put more energy into their performances than I had seen up to this point. Scott was asked to swing from a tree and crash into a pile of garbage, and he didn't even complain. When he emerged from the bags, he had a banana peel stuck to his shoulder. He laughed right along with the entire crew.

A good portion of the day was taken up filming an intense scene with Kirk, Pete, and Valerie. In it, Kirk was supposed to face off against Rock Bockner for the final time. They attempted to do the scene, but Pete started giggling for no reason at all. Then they tried again, and Pete did it again. Another take, and Pete smiled, making Kirk giggle. Soon, none of the actors could even speak a word without the cast and crew laughing uncontrollably. They did the scene 17 times before they finally got it right. But number 18 was perfect. And no one complained about numbers 1 through 17.

I was still laughing when Jill came up behind me. "I got it!" she exclaimed.

TEN

COMEBACK CITY OF THE YEAR

JILL PULLED ME INTO HER office and closed the door behind us. "I found the proof." She opened a folder. "I went to Alice to see if she had any of the evidence left from the trial, and she did. This." She held up a sheet of paper and I looked at it.

"The medical instruction sheet?"

"Right. From Dr. Yohman."

"It looks real."

"Sure it does. It's on letterhead, it has a lot of long, medical-sounding words on it, and it even has what looks like an adult's signature on it. But I know one of the secretaries at Dr. Yohman's office, so I called her. She told me that Jake is indeed a patient of theirs, but that he didn't come in at all on the day of the accident."

"Really?"

"And he hasn't been in since that day, either. But listen to this. He was in the office the day *before* the accident."

"For what?"

"She couldn't tell me that. But guess what he could've done while he was at the doctor's office?"

I was catching on. "Stolen some of their stationery."

"Exactly. Then he forged the doctor's signature thinking that nobody would check into it."

"Are you sure Jake never went into the doctor's office that day?"

"Positive."

"All right. Tell you what," I said. "I can't go with you, but go get Alice, then Jake. Then I think you should all pay a visit to Dr. Yohman."

• • •

Later on, I heard about what happened, and I wished I had been there. Alice pulled Jake out of his clubhouse by his ear. Jill said he didn't seem to be having any trouble with his ankle, which was interesting. Alice suggested handcuffs, but Jill thought that was a little over the top. So she simply pulled him by his arm to Dr. Yohman's office, which was only a few blocks away. Jake protested, but a quick ear pull from Alice shut him up. He mumbled something about police brutality, and Jill whispered to her to take it easy on him. He was, after all, someone who liked to sue.

Jill said Jake's eyes got wide when he discovered that their destination was Dr. Yohman's office. He figured out pretty quickly what was going to happen next. Jill asked the secretary if they could see the doctor for a minute. Then they all sat down—one big, happy family—in the waiting room. Jake squirmed in his seat the entire time.

The doctor came out and asked what this was all about.

"Dr. Yohman," Jill said.

"Yes?"

"Do you know Jake here?"

"Oh, yes. Hello, Jake. How are you doing?" Dr. Yohman said with a smile. Jake couldn't seem to return the smile.

"Jake had us believe that you diagnosed his condition as pulled ligaments in his ankle. In fact, he gave us this to prove it."

"This is not my signature."

"It's not?"

"That doesn't look anything like my signature. And what is this diagnosis? This doesn't make any sense. 'A stretched cardiac ligament on the anterior side of the ulna bone.' Cardiac refers to the heart, and the ulna is a bone in your arm."

"So, you didn't write this?"

"No. In fact, whoever *did* write it could be in a lot of trouble. Forging medical documents is against the law."

"Really? Wow."

Dr. Yohman got a call, and went back into his office. Jill looked at Jake. "So, Jake, do you have something to tell us?" Alice stepped forward and leaned down into his face, close enough to bite his nose if she'd wanted to.

• • •

Jake admitted to everything, except Max's involvement. I think he must have been scared of what Max might do to him if he ratted on him.

Alice and Jill interrogated Max anyway. Max told them he was just the lawyer, and lawyers have to defend innocent people, guilty people, and even sometimes people who fake injury to make money. He was "shocked" that Jake had lied to him.

Jake's crime was bad enough to earn him immediate banishment from the city. Jake was gone, never again to be a citizen of Kidsboro, and he had no idea that I had helped do it to him. It was perfect.

However, we couldn't lay any blame on Max. At least we'd discovered that the lawsuit was a fraud. Nelson's money was immediately returned to him, and right away, he went to Max's house to pay back his loan. As he said, "I don't want to be in debt to that snake any longer than I have to be." The next line of cars produced by Nelson Motors had four-wheel drive, air bags, antilock brakes, and even tiny little cup holders. They were the best cars yet.

• • •

I approached Jake cautiously as he was taking his stuff out of his clubhouse. He sneered at me. "I bet you're happy." I didn't answer.

"You might actually get a decent night's rest for once, huh?" I kept my mouth shut, but he kept talking. "I wouldn't get too comfortable, though. You know what I found out? Your dad left California. About a month ago."

What? My dad loved California. His job was there. *Why would he leave?*

"Nobody knows where he went," he chuckled. "Hey! Maybe he's on his way to find *you*." He turned away and chuckled again to himself. For a moment I had trouble breathing. What if he *was* trying to find us? And what if Jake had contacted him somehow?

Jake turned back around. "And don't worry, Jim. I'll be back."

• • •

I decided this had gotten too serious to keep to myself anymore, so I told my mom about Jake and his news that Dad had moved from California. I was afraid she would make us pack up and leave right then, but she suggested something else instead.

We got down on our knees next to my bed and prayed together for a long time. We asked for God's protection. We cried a little bit, but afterward I think we both felt better. We felt assured that God would take care of us, and for the first time since I'd seen Jake again, I was able to sleep peacefully.

• • •

Two weeks later, Kidsboro was back. Loans had been paid off, and the bank had plenty of reserve cash. The city council voted to create our version of a Federal Deposit Insurance Corporation (FDIC), which is a government organization that makes sure that if a bank runs out of money, the people who have their money in it don't lose it all.

The first thing each business owner did, once the business had made enough money, was pay off Max. He now owned only his wood shop. The golf course was renamed "Golf-O-Rama." Pete showed movies every night, and the theater flourished. But it never had a turnout like the night of nights . . .

• • •

I counted 55 people at the world premiere of *Rock Bockner and the Forest of Pain*. There were 29 citizens of Kidsboro, all except Max who was curiously absent, and 26 people from the outside. When Pete's parents walked between the hanging bed sheets and into the "theater," I introduced myself. They seemed just as excited as everyone else.

Valerie wore what looked like a prom dress, catching the eye of every boy she walked past. She smiled and greeted everybody.

Eugene Meltsner arrived carrying a thermos, and Pete made him leave it outside. No one was allowed to bring in outside drinks.

Connie Kendall, a teenage employee at Whit's End, came in just after Eugene. She said hi to everyone and told Pete how excited she was to see the movie.

Mr. Whittaker hugged a few people on his way in, and then he bought a giant bucket of popcorn at the concession stand to share with anyone who was sitting around him.

I sat down on a stump in the back. It was a gorgeous night. Jill came in and saw me, waved, and joined me on the stump. "This is gonna be so cool," she said.

"Yeah, it is," I agreed.

She looked around at the stars and the trees, and then closed her eyes. Her black hair flowed in the breeze like it was floating on water. She opened her eyes and looked at me. "You're not going to tell me what's going on, are you?" I knew she was talking about my relationship with Jake.

"One day I will."

"Do you need me to tell *you* something personal? Is that it? You want me to go first?"

"No, that's not it—"

"All right, I'll go first," she interrupted. "I think you're perfect."

"Perfect?"

"Pretty much. Except for all those nasty little secrets you keep. Other than that, you're flawless."

"That's . . . quite a compliment."

"It's not a compliment. Just an observation." She shrugged it off.

Pete walked to the front of the crowd, and before he could even start talking, everyone clapped. He blushed. He was wearing a suit. He thanked everyone and began his prepared speech.

"Thank you all for coming. Tonight is the result of all our hard work. So many creative minds came together to pull this off. To be honest, I think this movie ended up better than I ever dreamed it would be—and that's because of the people I worked with. I went into this thinking this was *my* production, *my* project, *my* creative genius that would make it all work . . . but it ended up being yours as well. This is *our* movie, and I'm proud to have been a part of it. I hope you feel the same way."

Everyone clapped, and the projector was flipped on and began to whir. Every eye was focused on Kirk as he came onto the screen and whispered his sinister plot to his partner. Some of the crowd hissed, and Kirk was elbowed by the people next to him near the front row. Valerie came on in the second scene and various whistles and cheers filtered through the audience. I could hear Valerie giggling.

The movie was 45 minutes long. The crowd laughed at the jokes that were only remotely funny and clapped at the points that were even barely inspirational. And when Rock Bockner defeated the evil villain, the audience sent up a loud roar of approval.

The acting was pretty bad, the script was weak, and the stunts were pitiful, but it was us, doing our thing.

Afterward, Pete led a discussion about the movie and declared it a classic. Everyone agreed, though many people did point out some of the less than logical things in the movie. Pete took it all in stride. We talked and laughed well into the night.

And no one wanted to go home.

THE END